Unforgettable

A BITTER CREEK NOVEL

JOAN JOHNSTON

UNFORGETTABLE

ISBN 978-0-9912507-9-0

www.joanjohnston.com

Interior Book Design by e-book-design.com
Cover Design by Nancy November Sloane, nancy-november.squarespace.com

Printed in the United States

L ydia felt groggy. She groaned as she stretched out on the luxurious hotel bed. She tried shoving the exquisitely soft Egyptian cotton sheets aside with her feet, but they were tangled in something that felt even more like silk. Which was when Lydia realized she was still wearing her ball gown.

She shoved herself upright and stared down at the wrinkled powder-blue silk, then gasped and put her hands to her throat in search of the priceless pearl necklace she'd worn to last night's masked charity ball at the *Boscolo Exedra Roma*, a magnificent five-star hotel in Rome.

It wasn't there.

The fabulous teardrop-shaped pearl, called the Ghost of Ali Pasha, had been worn over the centuries by sultans and queens, by kings and princesses. It had been given to her mother, Bella, Duchess of Blackthorne, by her father, billionaire banker Jonathan "Bull" Benedict, on the day of Lydia's birth.

Where had it gone?

Lydia's heart began to race, and the copper taste of fear rose in her throat as she frantically searched the bedding for the missing necklace. Perhaps the clasp had come undone. She jumped out of bed and teetered dizzily. She grabbed her head and groaned again. How many lemon drop martinis had she drunk last night?

She could only remember having two. So why was she feeling so dizzy and sick to her stomach? Why had she fallen asleep in her dress? And where, oh where, had she put the Ghost of Ali Pasha?

"Mother's going to kill me!" Especially since Lydia hadn't gotten permission to borrow the necklace in the first place.

She stumbled over her strappy heels, which lay on the floor beside the bed, and accidentally knocked everything off the end table. She dropped to her knees and desperately picked through the debris.

A crumpled Kleenex. A bottle of Delicious Red fingernail polish. She remembered chipping a fingernail and needing to repair it last night before the ball. The room key card. Her Kate Spade clutch purse, which was barely big enough for a few hundred euros, a tube of Raving Red lipstick and her iPhone.

No necklace.

She struggled to her feet and stumbled barefoot to the bathroom, tossing cosmetics around on the dressing table. Her head pounded at the clatter of glass against marble. The lingering, musky smell of Paloma Picasso perfume made her nauseous. She found a pair of diamond earrings and an emerald bracelet, but no pearl necklace.

She staggered out into the sitting room of her elegant suite on the Piazza Trinita dei Monti, at the top of the Spanish Steps, holding on to the antique furniture as she went, her gaze leaping from surface to surface. She threw the flowered pillows off the sofa, then yanked off the cushions to see if the necklace might have fallen behind or beneath them.

Nothing.

Lydia's moan became a wail of despair. How could she have been so careless? Her eldest brother, Oliver, Earl of Courtland, had arranged for her to receive the necklace from the vault at Blackthorne Abbey near London where her mother's precious jewels were stored. She'd promised him that the priceless necklace would be kept in the Hotel Hassler safe every moment it wasn't around her neck.

How was she going to explain her actions to her mother—and to Oliver, who'd trusted her to act responsibly—if she couldn't find the Ghost? She knew for a fact that her father had spent $25 million on the precious jewels—diamonds, rubies, sapphires, and emeralds—that provided a frame for the enormous, irreplaceable teardrop pearl that was the centerpiece of the necklace.

She'd received $50 million in a trust fund this past year when she'd turned twenty-five, but she'd invested the money with the Castle Foundation, founded by her four older brothers to do good works. All she had left was a quarterly allowance.

How would she ever make amends for the loss?

Oliver had told her that if she could get permission from their mother to borrow the Ghost, he would make the necessary arrangements to get the necklace to Rome. Lydia had been so sure the duchess would say "No" that she'd never asked. She'd simply told Oliver she had permission. And he'd believed her.

She could never have imagined the disaster that had occurred. Never imagined that the necklace would disappear from around her neck without a trace. Lydia groaned like a dying animal. She idolized her eldest brother. Oliver was going to hate her. Far worse, he was never going to trust her again.

Lydia turned in a circle in the elegant sitting room, with its marble arches and panoramic views of the Eternal City visible through the tall, brocade-curtained windows. "Where is it?" she cried. "Where could it be?"

She felt a sudden burst of hope as a thought came to mind. Maybe she'd dropped the necklace off at the hotel safe on the way up to her room. That made perfect sense. She grabbed the phone and called the front desk. A glance at the sun shining in from the balcony through the open curtains told her it must be almost noon. She never slept that late. How much *had* she drunk?

She remembered having a wonderful time at the masked ball, especially since her mask and costume allowed her to elude the titled gentleman her father wanted her to marry. There was nothing essentially wrong with Harold Delaford,

Earl of Sumpter, son and heir of the Marquess of Tenby. He was nice. He practically doted on her. And he was determinedly courting her.

But kissing Harold was like kissing a leather-bound book. There was simply no thrill. There had been no challenge in making Harold—he disliked being called Harry—fall in love with her. He'd been besotted at first glance, as so many men were.

Lydia couldn't help the fact that she'd been genetically blessed with both beauty and brains. She had her mother's violet eyes, ivory complexion, and lush figure and her father's black hair, strong chin, and mathematical genius. She had the added bonus of being British royalty as Lady Lydia, daughter of the Duchess of Blackthorne. Lord Delaford expected her to be seen on his arm, but not heard, like some fragile Victorian doll, kept on the shelf, admired but not touched.

She wanted more. She didn't know what, exactly. She yearned for passion. For adventure. For a life that was challenging and romantic and full of surprises. Was that so much to ask? She'd spent most of her life in one British or European boarding school after another, since she managed to get herself thrown out on a regular basis for some mischief. But that was the extent of her brushes with bedlam.

She'd been creating her own excitement for the past six months by emulating the work Oliver did. Not that he knew she'd discovered his secret. Oliver spent his spare time discreetly retrieving stolen artifacts and returning them to their rightful owners. He was currently in Argentina seeking a Russian triptych stolen by the Nazis. She was on a similar quest here in Rome but having considerably less success.

"This is Lydia Benedict," she said when the hotel receptionist answered the phone. "Can you check your records to see whether I returned anything to the safe late last night?"

"I'll check for you, Lady Lydia," a voice replied in Italian.

Lydia hadn't even realized she was speaking Italian. That was the problem with being multi-lingual. "Thank you," she said in British-accented English. She'd probably dropped the necklace off before she'd come upstairs. Surely she had. That was why it wasn't around her neck. It was lying in its black velvet box in the hotel safe.

"You last signed for your box at seventeen hundred hours four minutes, my lady."

Lydia sank onto the sofa, losing her balance when she landed on the low, hard frame, rather than the cushions, which she'd tossed onto the floor. She remembered retrieving the necklace from the safe around 5:00 p.m. the previous evening and coming upstairs to dress for the ball. "Is there any chance I might not have signed in when I gave an item to you for safekeeping?" she asked hopefully.

"No chance at all, Miss Benedict."

"*Grazi*," she said as she disconnected the phone. "No no no no no no no no," she muttered. "This can't be happening."

But it was. It had.

What was she going to do? She couldn't bear to see the look

on her mother's face the next time she saw her, or on Oliver's face at the next quarterly meeting of the Castle Foundation.

What about Mother's feelings when she discovers the Ghost is missing? The Ghost was a love gift from Father. She'll be devastated at its loss.

Sometimes it was difficult to imagine her mother having feelings. Or being in love. The Duchess of Blackthorne was always so cool and composed, even around her children. Especially around her children. Except, as the youngest of five and the only girl, Lydia knew it was all an act. She'd seen her mother weeping bitterly. She'd seen the forlorn look on the duchess's face after one of Bull and Bella's many violent arguments before their separation ten years ago.

Lydia was sure her mother still loved her father. Otherwise she wouldn't have cried such hopeless tears over their separation. Lydia shuddered when she remembered what had happened when she'd tried to comfort her mother.

It hadn't been easy reaching out to the duchess. She'd always been a distant mother. Lydia had come home to Blackthorne Abby from boarding school in Switzerland for a short vacation and had barely seen her parents during the visit. She'd always yearned to be closer to her mother, and she couldn't help wanting to comfort someone in as much pain as her mother seemed to be.

Lydia had barely laid a hand on her mother's shoulder when the duchess whipped around and confronted her with an angry look. The duchess already had her mouth open to chastise the intruder when she realized it was Lydia. "Oh."

That was all her mother said. Not "I could use a hug" or "Come here, sweetheart" or "Thank you for caring." What she'd finally said was, "I need to be alone."

Alone with her pain. That was how Lydia imagined her mother had lived the past ten years without her father, alone at Blackthorne Abbey, the hereditary castle of the Dukes of Blackthorne in Kent, about an hour south of London. All alone. Except for all the paramours, of course, whose arm would be entwined with hers at whatever social or charity event her parents were inevitably both attending somewhere in the world.

Her father was no better. Equally distant. Equally remote from his children. He spent most of his time at the Paris office of his banking empire. Both parents had flaunted their lovers over the past ten years, creating great tabloid fodder and making Lydia's life at boarding school a nightmare—until she confronted the gossips with acid remarks about their own genealogy. That shut them up. At least until her parents' next flagrant public misbehavior.

Many times Lydia had wished Bella and Bull would just get a divorce and be done with it. The gossips said her father refused to divorce her mother because he would be forced to split his fortune with her if they did. Lydia didn't for a moment think that was the reason they were still married. It was as obvious as the pain on both their faces that they were still deeply in love with each other. She often wondered what it was that had torn them apart and whether the breach could ever be mended.

Lydia felt her throat clogging with emotion. She was sorry to have lost her mother's necklace, but even more than her mother's censure, she dreaded the consequences Oliver might face for having given her the necklace in the first place. There had to be some way to figure out how and when the Ghost had disappeared.

"Of course!" she said, lurching from the sofa toward the bedroom and the pile of stuff she'd left on the floor.

Lydia located her iPhone and punched in a number that connected her with her mother's executive assistant, Emily Sheldon. Emily was in her early thirties, a slender woman with a homely face—that sounded cruel to say, but it was the absolute truth—warm brown eyes, a kind heart and a large, poverty-stricken family she seemed to be single-handedly supporting, both emotionally and financially.

Lydia had to tell someone what had happened. Emily had been Lydia's confidante more than once during the past three years since the young woman had become the duchess's assistant, and never once had she revealed any of the secrets Lydia had shared.

"Emily?" she choked out when the phone was answered.

"Lady Lydia? Is that you?" Emily asked.

Lydia struggled to hold back a sob. "I'm in trouble, Emily!"

"Where are you, Lydia? Are you all right? Do you need help?"

Lydia could tell Emily was upset because she'd forgotten

the "Lady" she always inserted before "Lydia." Emily was a stickler for the proprieties, even though neither Lydia, nor any of her siblings, cared whether they were addressed by their British titles. "No one can help," Lydia said at last.

"Let me call Lord Oliver—"

"Not Oliver!" Lydia cried. "I don't want him to know what's happened." Not until she had no other choice.

"Calm down," Emily said. "I won't contact Lord Oliver, if you don't want me to. Tell me where you are."

"Rome."

"Are you in danger?"

"Not exactly," Lydia replied.

Emily's British accent was clipped as she asked, "Are you in danger, my lady? Or not?"

Lydia half sobbed, half laughed and said, "Only from Mother. She's going to kill me when she finds out what I've done."

"The duchess loves you, Lady Lydia. There's nothing you can do that she won't forgive."

"Really?" Lydia said. "What do you think she'll say when she finds out I've lost the Ghost?"

Emily gasped.

There was no other sound from the other end of the line. At last Lydia said, "Emily? Are you still there?"

"What happened?" Emily asked, her voice surprisingly calm.

"I told Oliver I had Mother's permission to borrow the necklace, so he arranged to have it delivered to me in Rome. I wore it to a charity ball last night. Sometime during the night, the Ghost disappeared."

"From the hotel safe?" Emily asked.

"I didn't put it back in the safe."

"Oh, Lady Lydia."

Lydia heard the disapproval in the other woman's voice and said defensively, "When I got back to my hotel—" She realized she didn't know exactly when or even how she'd gotten back to her hotel room. That was a mystery she was going to have to unravel. It seemed safer, more honest, to simply say, "I never returned it to the safe."

"How long has the necklace been missing?"

"I don't know. I just woke up—it's a little after noon here in Rome—and discovered it wasn't around my neck or in the room or in the hotel safe. I couldn't believe it at first. I've been looking everywhere for what seems like hours. It isn't here."

"Please let me call Lord Oliver."

"No! Please, please, Emily. Don't tell Oliver. He thought I had permission to borrow the necklace. He'll get in trouble, too. I don't want him to know I lost it like this. He said I could keep it for ten days. There's another charity event coming up, and he said I could wear it for both. There's still time for me to find the Ghost before I'm supposed to return it. Once I find it, I can apologize to Mother, and to Oliver, for being so careless, but not until then."

Once again, Lydia heard silence on the other end of the line. She didn't know where to turn if Emily couldn't help her.

She held her breath waiting for her mother's capable assistant to come up with a solution to her dilemma.

At last Emily said, "I'm going to call someone to come and help you find the necklace. His name is Sam Warren. He's a private investigator from America, from Dallas, Texas, to be precise. He's the very best, Lydia. He should be there by tomorrow morning. Don't worry. If Sam can't find the Ghost, it can't be found.

"But it *has* to be found!"

Emily gave a shaky laugh. "What I meant to say is that Mr. Warren will find it. He's never failed on a mission your mother has given him yet."

"Thank you, thank you, thank you, Emily!" Lydia felt almost giddy with relief. "Let me know when his flight is arriving here in Rome, and I'll go meet it."

"Oh, dear. I don't think Sam will want your help."

"He doesn't have any choice," Lydia said with conviction. "I lost the Ghost. And I intend to be there when it's found."

CHAPTER 2

*S*amantha Warren paced the Mexican-tiled kitchen floor of her sprawling home in Dallas, her cell phone clutched in one hand. She chewed on a fingernail that was already bitten to the quick, shook her hand when she drew blood, and sucked on the wounded finger to ease the pain. She'd known this day was coming. She was only surprised it had taken two years for it to arrive.

The Duchess of Blackthorne's assistant, Emily Sheldon, had called with a new assignment, one which required the presence of the owner of Warren & Warren Investigations, Sam Warren, *in person*. The problem was, Samantha's father, Sam Warren, had been missing, and presumed dead, for two years.

Her father had disappeared while scuba diving near the Greek island of Santorini. After a brief investigation, the Greek authorities had concluded he'd drowned. Sam didn't buy it. Her father was a master diver, too careful in his preparations to have had a diving accident. And he was an Olympic silver medalist in distance swimming.

It seemed impossible that a man as competent and conscientious as her father could have drowned, disappearing without a trace. The authorities claimed he had. Her father's rented Chris-Craft had been discovered anchored near a small Greek island. No sign of him had ever been found.

Samantha had been twenty-four at the time and had been working for her father full-time since graduation from Texas Tech. She'd used all the investigative skills her father had taught her to search for him. Two years later, she was no closer to knowing what had happened to Sam Warren than she had been on the dreadful day she'd learned of his disappearance.

She'd clung tenaciously to the fragile hope that somehow, somewhere, her father was still alive. But if he was, why hadn't he contacted her? The only explanation that made any sense was that her father had been injured and had no memory of who he was. Which meant she was going to have to retrace his steps in Greece to find him.

That had been harder than she'd ever imagined, especially with all her responsibilities at Warren & Warren Investigations.

Most of her father's business had been devoted to keeping an eye on the Duchess of Blackthorne's four sons and daughter. Samantha had actually been the one responsible for the monthly reports to the duchess that had threatened to take up all of her father's time. When her father disappeared, she'd been afraid that if the duchess knew that Sam Warren's twenty-something daughter was taking over in his "temporary" absence, she'd shift her business to someone older and wiser.

So Samantha had hired a male assistant to be the "voice" of Sam Warren and pretended in her communications with the duchess that her father was still on the job.

With the crazy economy, and the increased demand over the past year for information about her five grown children, the Duchess of Blackthorne had become the *only* client of Warren & Warren Investigations. If the duchess discovered Samantha's deceit now, chances were that she would fire her for sure, which would effectively put Samantha out of business.

She wouldn't have cared, except she spent every penny she made, and all of her free time, searching for clues to what had happened to her father. Recently, she'd gotten the first promising lead she'd had since shortly after his disappearance. She needed the duchess's money to follow it all the way to Greece. Which meant she needed to keep Bella as a client.

That was why, come hell or high water, Sam Warren had to show up in Rome tomorrow morning. The only question was who Samantha should send, since she certainly couldn't show up herself.

The obvious person to go was Kevin Mortenson, the male PI Samantha had hired to impersonate her father if the duchess ever wanted to speak to Sam Warren on the phone. Because her father ran his business out of their home, Samantha had often been the one who'd answered the phone when the duchess or her assistant called while her father was still alive.

She'd continued to do so after his disappearance.

Luckily, between texting, email, and International Fed-Ex shipping, it had never once been necessary for Kevin to pretend to be her father. So Samantha was shocked when Kevin vehemently refused to go to Rome.

"No, Sam," he'd said, staring her down. "Not only no, but I'd rather burn in hell for eternity than fly to Rome and impersonate your dad."

"Why not?" she'd demanded. "That was the reason I hired you in the first place!"

"I know enough about the duchess now to fear what might happen to me if she ever found out the truth about what's been going on for the past two years."

Samantha scoffed. "What is it you think she's going to do?"

"That woman can be as ruthless as her eldest son, as heartless as her twin sister, and as unpredictable as her husband. That's a lethal combination. I don't have the first clue what she might do if she caught me pretending to be Sam Warren. And I don't intend to find out."

"What do you suggest I do?" Sam said, her balled fist stuck on one canted hip.

"Tell her the truth."

"But she might—"

"My point exactly," Kevin interrupted. "She might do something terrible. You got yourself into this mess. You can get yourself out."

Kevin stalked out without giving Samantha a chance to

beg. She was staring out the kitchen window at the tall hedge that was all that separated her from a nearby neighbor, fighting back tears, when she heard bottles rattling. She turned in time to see her brother Joe standing between the open refrigerator door and the shelves inside. He twisted the cap off a bottle of Heineken, then held himself steady with a hand on the door and brought the ice-cold beer bottle up to his lips.

Samantha stared, entranced, as he leaned his head back and swallowed down half of it. At thirty, Joe was only four years older than she was, but he had the ageless gaze of an old man, the result of violent years spent as a member of the army's elite Delta Force. Master Sergeant Joseph Samuel Warren had received a medical discharge six months ago due to a catastrophic injury to his right leg from an IED—an improvised explosive device—in Afghanistan.

Once a powerful, broad-shouldered six foot two, her brother was now mostly ribs. A jagged white scar angled down the right side of his face, cutting through brow and cheekbone all the way to his chin. Before her stood a shadow of the proud soldier who'd left for Afghanistan less than a year ago.

Samantha had allowed Joe to brood—and drink—because she'd thought he would get over his bitterness in a few days or weeks and move on with his life. But the more self-pity he'd displayed at being forced out of a job he loved—and losing a fiancée who didn't bargain for a disabled, scarred, and jobless husband—the less sorry she'd felt for him.

Joe was still drinking six months after his discharge, with

no signs of stopping. His light-blue eyes were bloodshot, his face was covered with a rough stubble of dark beard, and his military buzz cut had long since grown out, lank black hair hanging over his forehead.

When his Adam's apple had finished bobbing, he scratched his gaunt belly, belched loudly, stepped back so he could shove the refrigerator door closed, and asked in a slurred voice, "What's for supper?"

Samantha's green eyes narrowed on her brother. Instead of the sallow-faced drunk standing in her kitchen, she imagined the tanned, muscular, skillful—and dangerous—Delta Force operative Joe used to be. Maybe she could kill two birds with one stone. Why not send Joe? It would give him something to do that would get him out of the house and away from the bottle. And it would provide her with a "Sam Warren" to help Lydia Benedict find the Ghost.

"You don't have time for supper," she said, suddenly making up her mind.

"Why not?"

"You've got to catch a flight to Rome."

His eyes widened in surprise. Then he grinned, revealing very white, very straight—thanks to several years in braces he'd hated—teeth. "Is this a joke?"

It was a wicked smile, one that had made her girlfriends sigh and wish that Joe would look in their direction. Hopefully, that smile would keep Lydia Benedict distracted long enough for Samantha to find the missing Ghost of Ali Pasha.

Once Samantha had located the apparently stolen jewel, which was too well-known not to be talked of in the black market, she could send Joe to retrieve it, something she was certain he could manage.

"No joke," she said brusquely. "I need you to fly to Rome tonight for a case I'm working on."

"I'm going back to bed." He staggered as he turned, accidentally putting weight on a leg that could no longer hold him all by itself. He caught himself with a palm smacked against the wall, then limped back toward the hallway that led to his bedroom.

"I need your help, Joe."

That stopped him in his tracks. He leaned most of his weight on his good leg and kept a hand on the wall to ease the strain on his injured limb. "I can't help you, Sam. I can't help anyone," he said bitterly.

Samantha hurried to catch her brother before he could move again. She grabbed his arm and was astonished when she felt rock-hard muscles tense at her touch. She'd noticed Joe doing push-ups, pull-ups, and sit-ups every morning, but she hadn't paid much attention to his workouts. Apparently he was a lot more fit than his bloodshot eyes and gaunt ribs suggested.

Joe kept his head down and his eyes averted as she pleaded, "The duchess expects Sam Warren *in person* to show up in Rome to track down a priceless pearl necklace, called the Ghost of Ali Pasha, that's been stolen. Kevin won't go. If you don't help me, she's going to find out the truth. And I'm going to be out of business."

"You made your bed—" he began.

"Yes, I did," she said fiercely. "Because I was afraid the duchess wouldn't keep using Dad's business to investigate her children's activities if she knew it was just me. But I've finally got a decent lead on what happened to Dad in Greece. I need the money the duchess pays me to follow it."

Joe scratched the short growth of whiskers under his chin with his free hand and glanced at her from the corner of his eye. "I'm not going to be much use in any kind of fight. This bum leg won't support me."

"You're not going to have to fight anyone," she assured him. "I just need someone to be Sam Warren while I investigate the theft of the Ghost."

"I'm too young to pass for Dad."

Samantha grimaced. "You're a better choice than me. And I don't have anyone else to send." She hesitated, then added, "There's a slight hitch."

His lips quirked. "There always is."

She gave him the bad news quickly. "The duchess's daughter, Lady Lydia, wants to help look for the Ghost. You'll be spending most of your time in Rome with her."

"No way," he said flatly. "I don't need some rich bitch spoiled brat ordering me around."

Samantha wasn't certain whether Lydia was a bitch or not, but she certainly was rich and spoiled. Not as rich as she had been before she'd donated her trust fund to the Castle Foundation. Nevertheless, the allowance Lydia got from the foundation allowed her to maintain her wealthy lifestyle.

Samantha felt a moment's hesitation when she imagined the pampered young woman interacting with her nuts-and-bolts, no-nonsense brother. But she had no choice. "Lydia didn't have permission from her mother to borrow the Ghost, even though she told her brother—who retrieved the necklace for her from the vault in England where it was stored—that she did."

Joe shook his head in disbelief.

"Now she's worried that Oliver will blame her for losing it."

"She did lose it."

"The Ghost isn't the sort of thing you 'lose.' More likely, it was stolen from her."

"I don't know squat about recovering lost jewels," Joe said flatly.

"I'll do the investigating," Samantha said. "I just need you to be a body in place."

Joe scowled. "That's about all I'm good for now."

Samantha hated the despair she heard in her brother's voice. She was determined to get Joe on that plane to Rome. He needed to start thinking about the future instead of reliving the glories of a past that was gone forever.

"I talked with Lydia briefly," she continued, "and she has no memory of how she got home from the charity ball where she wore the necklace or much of anything else that happened."

"Rohypnol," Joe said brusquely. He turned and leaned his back against the wall, taking all the weight off his bad leg.

"Do you want to sit down?" Samantha asked with concern.

Joe shook his head. "I'm fine. Go on."

She could see he was in pain. It was his own fault. The doctors had told him that too much muscle was gone from his right calf and thigh for the leg ever to do the job it was supposed to do. They'd been convinced he would never walk again on a leg with so much damage, and that if he did somehow manage to walk, he would always need a cane. They'd wanted to amputate and give Joe a prosthetic device. He'd fought to keep his mutilated leg.

The doctors had also warned him that the lacerated muscle tissue would continue to cause him pain long after it had healed.

But Joe had been adamant. "Leave the leg where it is."

When he'd gotten out of Brooke Army Medical Center in San Antonio, he'd been a crazy man, exercising his leg until he had horrible cramps. But it had never gotten strong enough to bear his entire weight on its own. He'd proved the doctors partly wrong. He was walking again. Limping, rather. But her brother's strained features made it plain that the doctors had been right about the pain—except that what he suffered was far worse than mere pain. He could only avoid the excruciating cramps by consistently using a cane to take the weight off his injured leg.

Which, of course, he refused to do.

So he suffered. And raged at the circumstances that had taken away his mobility and the work he loved. And drank to blot out the pain, both physical and emotional.

He'd paid a price for his stubbornness. He wasn't the same powerful, confident, glass-is-overflowing man he'd been before his injury.

Samantha eyed her brother, wondering exactly how she should phrase her plea. She needed him to work with Lydia. She didn't want Lydia complaining later to her mother that Sam Warren hadn't let her help. "Lydia might be a little spoiled—"

Joe made a disgusted sound in his throat.

Samantha hurried on. "But she's more naive than anything else. With four older brothers, and being the only girl, she's been indulged and protected her entire life. She probably couldn't imagine someone daring to drug her drink."

Joe lifted a brow. "Is the Ghost the only thing she lost when she was drugged?"

"If you're asking if she was sexually assaulted after she was dosed with whatever was put in her drink, I don't believe so," Samantha said. "I asked, and Lydia said she was still wearing her clothes, down to her underwear, when she woke up, and she doesn't have any cuts or bruises that would suggest an attack."

The young woman had been surprised at the question and startled at the thought that she might have been drugged. She'd admitted that she rarely got drinks for herself, that some man or another was always bringing one to her. She didn't remember having a drink handed to her by a stranger, but everyone at the ball had been masked. Even if a stranger had handed her a drugged drink, she wouldn't have seen his face.

The fact that Lydia hadn't been personally attacked after she'd been drugged was a blessing. But Lydia's inability to remember what had happened the night of the masked ball left Samantha with a lot of unanswered questions and a lot of investigating to do.

"You're going to have to deal with Lydia," she told her brother. "She insists on being involved in the recovery of the stolen necklace."

"Talk her out of it."

"I've already tried," Samantha admitted. "It didn't work. Honestly, she might be able to help."

"A spoiled princess is going to help?" Joe said with a sneer. "How? By putting a jeweled crown on her head and demanding the bad guys hand over the goods?"

Samantha wouldn't have put it past Lydia to do exactly that, if she thought it would work. The girl was both intelligent and resourceful. And beautiful. Men were often struck dumb when they saw her for the first time. But she didn't think those arguments would improve her brother's attitude toward the privileged young woman.

So she said, "Lydia's been doing a lot of investigating herself over the past few months, looking for a stolen painting. She's not a complete novice, although her methods aren't too subtle."

"Why don't you go and work with this Lydia person yourself?" Joe asked. "That seems like the best solution all around."

Samantha shook her head. "I can't take the chance that

the duchess will fire me. A *man* named Sam Warren has to show up. I can't lose this job, Joe. In a couple of months I'll have enough to finance a trip to Greece to figure out what happened to Dad. Just help me out this once, and I promise I'll never ask again."

Samantha waited with bated breath until Joe said, "Just this once."

She gave him a quick hug and said in a choked voice, "Thank you!"

He shoved himself off the wall and hugged her tight for a moment before he let her go. "You realize I don't have any civvies."

His civilian clothes were at his home near Fort Bragg, the army camp in North Carolina where he'd last been posted. He'd shown up in Dallas wearing cammies and carrying his B-4 bag and hadn't left the house since.

"You can take the insignia off a set of cammies to wear on the plane and buy what you need when you get to Rome," Samantha said.

"I won't need much."

"You need a shave. And you need to be clear-eyed to deal with Lydia. She's no dummy, Joe. And she's extraordinarily beautiful."

He smirked. "Of course she is."

"Watch yourself." He would only get hurt if he let himself fall for Lydia. She was British royalty, and she was practically engaged to a marquess's son. She seemed to have no more use for a man who professed to love her than she had for a used tissue. Samantha didn't want her brother losing his heart to the duchess's daughter. He had enough wounds to recover from as it was.

Not that Joe was a saint in the love-'em-and-leave-'em department. Before he'd gotten engaged, he'd gone through a great many women. Unfortunately, the one he'd chosen to give his heart to had abandoned him when the chips were down. Her brother was a lot less likely to lose his heart again anytime soon. And he was sure to be cynical of the next woman who made the mistake of falling in love with him.

"You can sleep on the flight," Samantha continued. "No drinking on the plane, Joe, do you hear? I want you sober when you land."

"I might need a hair of the dog."

"No hair of any dog. No beer, no whiskey, no nothing," Samantha insisted. "And don't forget, when you meet Lydia Benedict, your name is *Sam.*"

CHAPTER 3

*L*ydia usually did her flying in the family jet, so she'd never spent much time standing around in Rome's Leonardo da Vinci Fiumincino Airport. She watched a pair of *carabinieres* dressed in sharp-looking dark blue uniforms with a red stripe down each leg as they approached a backpacker sleeping on a bench. One of the Italian policemen prodded the young man with his Uzi.

The bearded young man awoke with a start, took one look at the Uzis the policemen carried, grabbed his backpack from the bench where he'd been sleeping, and hurried away.

Are Uzis really necessary in a place as beautiful as this airport? Lydia shuddered. The more she traveled on her own, the more she was learning how precarious life could be. Someone had drugged her. Someone had stolen the Ghost. The world was a much more frightening place this morning than it had been yesterday.

She glanced over her shoulder and saw that the man who'd accosted her in the airport VIP lounge was still following her. She wondered if she should say something to the *carabinieres*. She glanced toward them, but they'd already moved off in the opposite direction. She would have felt silly running after them to complain that a well-dressed young man had told her how beautiful she was.

Yesterday, she would have smiled and accepted the compliment. Today, she didn't trust the Italian's intentions. She'd told him she preferred to be alone, but he'd sat down in a chair near her anyway. He was polished and charming and wouldn't take no for an answer. She'd always been able to handle the most aggressive males with aplomb. For some reason, this morning she couldn't find the right mix of courtesy and coldness to discourage him.

Finally, she'd given up and left the lounge. She was anxious to meet Sam Warren and get started looking for the Ghost. The bold Italian, with his exquisitely tailored suit and gold ring bearing a family crest, had followed her. He seemed to think she was playing some game with him.

Lydia wanted to lash out at him to leave her alone, but she'd been taught from birth that a lady never lost her temper. And she was a lady from the top of the French twist in her silky black hair to the tips of her red, four-inch-high Jimmy Choo heels.

She determinedly ignored the suave Italian, which only seemed to encourage him.

"*Tu sei bella*," he said, taking a step closer.

He'd merely told her she was beautiful, but she felt a frisson of unaccountable fear. She told herself her would-be suitor was merely a handsome man, like many others who'd sought her attention, but the events of the previous day had changed everything. She was suddenly terrified of the unknown.

Before she could turn to her tormentor, she heard a gruff male voice demand, "Are you Lydia Benedict?"

Lydia gaped at the tall, dangerous-looking hoodlum with sunken eyes, a dark beard, and shaggy black hair who'd stopped a foot in front of her. She blurted, "How do you know my name?"

He pointed to a sign she held down at her side—similar to those used by chauffeurs to locate their clients—which read SAM WARREN. She'd forgotten she was holding it.

"I was told to meet Lydia Benedict," he said. "I figured from the sign that you were waiting for me."

She was both confused and upset to find herself suddenly sandwiched between the two strangers. She wasn't sure which man provided the greater threat, the one dressed in an expensive Italian suit or the one staggering drunkenly before her in military desert camouflage.

"I'm Warren," the unshaven man said.

Lydia was appalled as she stared into his inscrutable ice-blue—and bloodshot—eyes. This was her help? This was the great Sam Warren? She'd been expecting someone much older. And more sober.

"I'm Lydia Benedict," she said at last. "You're my mother's private investigator?" She made it a question, still not quite believing this barbarian worked for the Duchess.

His mouth turned down, almost in disgust, as he repeated, "I'm Warren."

"I was expecting someone older."

"You got me."

Her nose wrinkled in distaste. "I don't think you—" At that moment, the Italian laid a possessive hand on her shoulder. Before she could protest, Sam Warren grabbed the Italian's wrist, jerked him forward, and back-heeled his feet out from under him. As the Italian landed hard on the marble floor, Warren stumbled and almost fell.

Lydia automatically reached out to steady him and felt a large male hand graze her right breast and brush across the nipple. She gasped at the intimate touch, but the huge hand had already found its way to her shoulder.

"Lost my balance," he said. "War wound."

Lydia took another—astonished—look at the man before her.

What she saw was a drunken male in army fatigues but with hidden strengths like power and agility and quickness. Was it possible this ruffian was good at solving crimes, like the theft of the Ghost? Even if he was, what about that "accidental" touch? Was she going to have to fight off the private investigator's unwanted attentions while they searched for the missing necklace?

Lydia eyed Sam Warren askance, trying to judge whether he'd merely stumbled or whether he'd actually had the nerve to feel her up in public. One look at his scarred face told her he'd been in battle. He'd certainly put that Italian in his place. When Warren took a step back, she realized he had a limp and bore most of his weight on one leg.

So perhaps the invasive touch had not been planned.

Nevertheless, she flushed. The rough-looking Texan's unexpected caress had managed to arouse her more than her would-be fiancé's ever had. She stared at the infamous Sam Warren, wondering if the Duchess had ever seen him in this condition.

His breath, when he'd fallen against her, had smelled of whiskey. His hair was unkempt, his cheeks and chin shadowed by dark beard, his clothes rumpled. He looked disreputable.

On the other hand, the military shirt and camouflage trousers did nothing to conceal a body that was broad in the shoulder, lean in the hip, and unbelievably strong.

That last part she knew not only from how easily he'd put the Italian on the ground but from having put her hands on him to keep him from falling. Her palm had landed on a belly that was rippled with taut muscle, and her hand had gripped a bicep that felt more like stone than human flesh. And yet, he had trouble standing on his own. She wondered if that was more a result of the war wounds or the whiskey.

The Italian chose that moment to sit up.

"Stay down," the hoodlum, who apparently, unbelievably, was her mother's private investigator, said in a harsh voice.

The man on the ground took one look at the primitive warrior standing over him and did as he was told.

"You have a car?" the drunken man asked her.

"Of course."

He started walking toward the doors that led to the street.

Lydia hesitated only an instant before she hurried after him, her Jimmy Choos tapping on the marble floor. "Wait!"

He didn't slow down, but his limp made it possible for her to catch up. "I need the best help I can get, Mr. Warren. You can barely keep yourself upright."

He stopped abruptly but near enough to a glass wall of windows to put a hand out to hold himself upright. He turned to her like a dog-baited bear and said, "I'm what you've got, lady. Take it or leave it. I'd be more than happy to turn around and get right back on that plane."

She was angry enough to send him back to Dallas. But then what would she do? She didn't know anyone she could trust with the fact that the Ghost was missing. The loss of such a priceless gem would be a tremendous scoop for the tabloids. She couldn't be sure that anyone else she hired wouldn't sell her secret to those vultures. The way things went viral on the Internet, her parents would know thirty minutes later that she'd lost the Ghost.

"I need your help," she said at last. "Where do we start?"

"I need some sleep."

Her eyes went wide in disbelief. "You didn't sleep on the plane?"

"I was too busy drinking."

He was totally unapologetic about arriving drunk and disheveled, Lydia realized. He didn't seem to realize the urgency of the situation.

"Do you have a bed I can use or not?"

"Where are you staying?"

"I didn't make a reservation, just got on the plane and came to Rome. You called and here I am."

Yes, here he was. A crippled drunk. She stopped herself right there. His bad leg hadn't stopped him from putting that Italian on the ground.

Perhaps the best move was to take him to the Hotel Hassler and clean him up. Maybe he would show to better advantage when he was sober and shaved.

Or maybe not. Maybe it would be better to throw herself on her mother's mercy. She caught her lower lip in her teeth. Not necessarily the best option when the Duchess had a reputation for being merciless.

Lydia slid the straps of her Gucci handbag higher up on her shoulder. She'd never been very good at facing consequences. Being rich and beautiful and smart had allowed her to avoid taking responsibility for a great many wrongs she'd done in the past. Somehow, she didn't think she'd escape unscathed if she gave up the hunt and simply admitted that she'd lost the Ghost.

It would be humiliating to have her dishonesty exposed to her brother. Humbling to admit her deception to her mother.

She shifted the placard containing Sam Warren's name in her hands, uncertain what to do. Should she toss it, and him, or hang on?

Warren shrugged and turned to leave.

"Wait!" she cried.

He stopped and glanced back over his shoulder.

"Can you really help me find the Ghost?"

"That's why I'm here, ma'am," he replied with an ironic twist of his lips.

It irked her to be called "ma'am," but she bit back a retort. Her restraint was wasted, because he'd already turned his back on her and started walking, or rather limping, away again. She realized he hadn't retrieved a single piece of luggage. It seemed he'd left Texas with nothing but the clothes on his back.

The inestimable Sam Warren made his way, half limping, half staggering toward the exit, apparently expecting her to follow.

Totally exasperated, she dumped the placard in the nearest trash can and hurried after him. "I would prefer that you call me Lydia," she said. "What should I call you, Mr. Warren?"

He glanced back, focused his bloodshot blue eyes on her, and said, "Call me Joe."

CHAPTER 4

*J*oe figured he must really have tied one on last night. His head ached and his mouth felt dry as desert-boot leather. He looked around for the woman who'd likely spent the night with him, considering he'd woken up naked in a powder-blue-silk-canopied bed made up with matching powder-blue silk sheets. Funny, he didn't feel sexually sated.

He rose slowly because his head hurt, but also to give the muscles in his injured leg time to warm up. When he moved the injured calf, a sharp pain shot all the way to his hip. He hissed a profanity. *This is your life,* he thought. *Pain. Forever and ever, Amen.*

He would have stayed where he was, but he needed to take a piss. He gritted his teeth as he used his hands to ease his bad leg over the edge of the bed. He probably should have had the damned thing cut off when he'd had the chance. He sat waiting for the stabbing pain to recede as he scouted the room for furniture he could lean on as he hobbled his way to the john. Maybe it was time to get a cane.

He balked at the thought. He wasn't a cripple.

Like hell you're not! Look at yourself. Go ahead. Look.

He glanced down at his ruined calf muscle. Ugly red gouges remained where flesh had been burned out by molten steel. He stood, putting weight on the leg, and bit back a yelp as he dropped onto the bed again. Damned thing hurt like a son of a bitch.

He heard a woman speaking Italian in the next room. Where the hell was he? He glanced around the upscale bedroom. Whoever the chick was, she was high end.

Then he remembered. And groaned. He was in Rome pretending to be Sam Warren, PI, at the invitation of the stunningly beautiful woman he'd met at the airport. He rubbed his bleary eyes and groaned again when he remembered how he'd told the lady to call him *Joe*, after his sister had warned him to use the name *Sam*. Too late now. The damage was done.

He wondered how long he'd been out. The curtains weren't completely closed, and from the angle of the sun, it looked like it was late afternoon. Apparently he'd slept the day away.

Miss High-and-Mighty had brought him back to her hotel room and tried to talk him into starting the search for her missing jewel right away. If he hadn't anesthetized his leg with Jack Daniel's on the long flight over the ocean, he might have given in to the entreaty in those amazing eyes of hers.

Lady Lydia Benedict was gorgeous. Stunning, really. He'd

felt his heart jump when he'd gotten his first look at her as he left customs. She was almost too perfect. Flawless skin, so creamy he'd wanted to lick it. Full strawberry lips that made him wonder how she'd taste. And those violet eyes, both innocent and . . . wary? No wonder, with some Italian lothario on her heels.

He'd wanted to kill the bastard for laying a pilfering hand on her. He'd put the guy on the ground, but he'd forgotten about his bad leg, lost his balance, and nearly ended up falling on his ass. Fortunately, Miss High-and-Mighty had saved him that ignominy.

But not before his hand had brushed against a soft breast and a surprisingly taut nipple. Her eyes had been indignant when she thought he'd copped a feel, then questioning, when he'd started to fall. He felt his body throb at the memory of how good she'd felt. Which reminded him he needed to take a leak. He dreaded the pain when he finally tried walking on his leg, so he put it off a few moments longer.

Joe couldn't believe he'd let his sister talk him into this harebrained scheme. He remembered reminding Samantha before he'd boarded the plane that he had no idea how to find a missing jewel. She'd assured him that she would do all the research to see who was bidding on the jewel, or where it might be transported, and get back to him. Supposedly, all he had to do was be a body in place. A wrecked body in place, he amended sourly.

Samantha should have told the Duchess of Blackthorne

that Sam Warren had disappeared, and that she'd been doing all the investigative work over the past couple of years.

Joe swore as he realized he was supposed to have called his sister the moment he arrived. He'd turned his phone off on the plane and hadn't turned it back on. He'd left the phone in the pocket of his cammie trousers, which he'd dropped on the lush carpeting when he'd stripped and toppled into bed. A quick look revealed his pants, along with the rest of his clothes, were gone.

"What the hell?" he muttered.

Another look revealed the contents of his pockets—wallet, passport, phone, chewing gum, and paper clip—scattered on the bedside table. The paper clip was a weapon, about all he could get past the TSA these days.

Maybe the Brit had sent his clothes out to be laundered or something. He'd been planning to buy something to wear anyway. He grabbed his cell phone, turned it on, and saw there were eight messages, about one an hour, from his sister. He ignored them and punched in the number Samantha had programmed for him.

"About time!" she said after a single ring. "Where have you been?"

She sounded worried. Hell. He was a grown man, a former Delta sergeant. She didn't need to worry about him.

"Joe?" she prodded.

He was embarrassed to admit the truth. "I was sleeping."

"You were supposed to call when you landed."

"I didn't. So what's going on? Have you located the pearl?"

"The Ghost is a ghost," Samantha said, sounding miserable. "There hasn't been a peep out of whoever took it, no sign of it on the black market, no sign of anything."

"That doesn't sound good."

"Maybe the thief is traveling."

"Let's hope not. Otherwise, I've wasted my time coming to Rome. What do you want me to do?"

"Have you had a chance to question Lady Lydia?"

"No."

"Then you should do that. You need to find out—"

"I think I can manage an interrogation," he interrupted.

"Don't *interrogate* her. *Question* her. She's a lady, Joe."

"I noticed."

"Don't notice her. Don't get any ideas at all about her. She lives in a different stratosphere," she warned.

"Got it," he said. "Is that all?"

"I'll be in touch if I get any info. Go back over everything Lady Lydia did the twenty-four hours before she lost the Ghost. If you discover anything useful, give me a call."

"Roger that."

"Take care of yourself," she said in a softer voice. "And whatever you do, don't fall for Lydia Benedict."

He didn't reply, just turned off the phone. He remembered the look on Lydia Benedict's face earlier that morning when she'd tried to talk him out of getting some rack time.

"We have to move fast," she'd said. "My brother—"

"I need sleep," he'd interrupted. He'd drunk enough on the plane to kill a horse—and a lot of pain. He was in no shape to do anything.

She'd tried batting her eyelashes at him. "Please. I need your help."

Her eyes were an odd shade between purple and blue, and he'd felt himself falling into them. He'd managed to say, "I know that probably works with most of the men you meet. I'm immune."

She'd stuck her hands on her hips and those beautiful violet eyes had flashed angrily.

He'd felt himself go hard as a rock and realized he was as susceptible to her wiles as any other red-blooded male, ready and willing to do whatever it took to please her—and get her flat on her back. He hadn't been hungry for a woman in a very long time. Right then he'd felt ravenous.

"You work for me," she'd snapped.

"I don't like bossy women."

"I'm not bossy, I'm your *boss*." She seemed to realize she was losing her cool, because she took a deep breath and let it out, then muttered, "If a savage like you is capable of telling the subtle difference between the two."

He'd have been happy to have her lead the way—in bed. Not much chance of that. She'd made it plain that she considered him a dumb brute. He'd crossed his arms to keep himself from pulling her into them and said, "I'm my own boss."

She was clearly desperate, because she laid a hand on his

forearm and said, in a sultry voice that made the hairs stand up on the back of his neck, "Please."

A shaft of desire shot like an arrow through his body. "Look, lady," he said, his voice harsh with sexual need, "I'm going to be a lot more useful to you when my head is clear." Which it sure as hell wasn't. He felt off-kilter with her standing so close.

He could smell some kind of flowery stuff in her hair, which was tied up tight on the back of her head. He'd wanted to let it down and sift his fingers through it and see if it was as soft and silky as it looked.

"Time is of the essence," she pleaded. "Couldn't you just make a few phone calls to whatever contacts you have?"

He realized he was ready to do anything she asked, go anywhere she wanted. The last time he'd been that vulnerable to a woman she'd walked away and left him high and dry. His heart still hurt from that fiasco. Better to nip this attraction in the bud.

"No, I can't," he'd said. "Good night."

"It's morning!" she'd shot back.

That had been eight hours ago. Joe winced as he stood, remembering how he'd backed up and firmly shut the bedroom door in her beautiful, incredulous face. Time to get moving. He took a step and nearly howled with pain.

He was trembling and covered with sweat by the time he made it to the bathroom. No wonder the army had kicked him out. No wonder his fiancée had left him. No wonder his sister had shoved him out of the house and onto that plane.

No wonder the most beautiful woman he'd ever met had looked at him with disdain.

"Aw, hell," he muttered. The likes of Lady Lydia Benedict was not for him. Besides, he wasn't going to give another woman a chance to kick him when he was down.

He was still peeing when he heard a crisp, British-accented male voice address the woman in the next room.

CHAPTER 5

*L*ydia realized that Sam Warren was finally awake when she heard the distinct sound of a male peeing like a racehorse. She grimaced. That was the sort of expression her mother abhorred and her father commonly used. Lydia tried to emulate the best of each of her parents, but too often she feared the opposite was true. She could never quite please either one of them.

Being both brainy and beautiful complicated everything. Beauty was a "get out of jail free" card for life. Men were awestruck. Women were envious. Both sexes gave her the benefit of the doubt when she got herself into trouble. And her family, well, as the baby of the lot, they gave her the greatest leeway of all.

Her brains made her judgmental of others, something she was ashamed of, and encouraged her to take risks, because she was so certain she could think her way out of any trouble she got herself into.

There was no thinking herself out of the situation she was in now. What she'd done this time, taking the Ghost without permission and then losing it, was beyond the pale. Her mother would be furious. Her father would be disappointed. Her eldest brother, Oliver, would chastise her. And the rest of her brothers—Riley, Payne, and Max—would laugh at her.

She hated being laughed at. Their laughter was dismissive, as though their little sister was of no account. She'd tried so hard to be more than beautiful, to use her intelligence to do something productive, but she didn't have much to show for twenty-five years of living. She stared in the direction of the noise still coming from the other room.

For heaven's sake! Couldn't the man have closed the bathroom door? Sam Warren was crude, rude, and disgusting.

And her only hope.

She'd been waiting all day for the Texan to wake up, praying he'd have some idea where she should start her search for the Ghost, because she couldn't think of a single place to look. She wondered why Warren had asked her to call him *Joe*, when his name was *Sam*, but decided it must be some American nickname. She'd thought he would be older, but apparently not. According to her mother's personal assistant, this Joe Warren character was an exceptional private investigator.

Lydia had her doubts. She rose from the sofa, where she'd been watching the latest news on the TV in Italian, and headed toward the bedroom to confront the American PI. She was interrupted by a knock at her hotel room door and hurried to answer it, since she was expecting the delivery of several packages. When she opened the door, she found an unwelcome guest.

Her escort to the masked ball the previous evening, Harold Delaford, Earl of Sumpter, son and heir of the Marquess of Tenby, stood before her, holding an exquisite bouquet of violets.

"Hello, Harry," she said, standing in the doorway to block his entrance.

"It's Harold," he corrected with a smile that revealed very white, if slightly crooked, front teeth. "These are for you."

The first time they'd met, Harold Delaford had remarked that her eyes reminded him of violets. Ever since, he'd brought her violets whenever he came calling.

"What do you want, Harold?"

He handed her the small bouquet and stepped into the room past her, as though she weren't standing in his way trying to keep him out. "Why haven't you answered any of my calls?"

Because I've lost the Ghost of Ali Pasha. "I've been busy," she said. "You can't stay, Harold."

He turned and flipped the privacy lock on the door, then added the bolt that guaranteed no one would interrupt them. "We need to talk."

"What do you think you're doing?"

"I believe I deserve an answer to the question I asked you at the ball," the earl said.

Lydia lifted her chin. "What question was that?"

Harold dropped to one knee in front of her, which revealed the small bald spot at the top of his head. "Does this ring any bells?"

She hated herself for caring whether Harold still had all his hair. Really, the hair wasn't the problem. It was the man wearing it. Harold was arrogant to the point of being unkind to lesser mortals like waiters and housemaids. He was too wealthy for his own good, and good-looking enough, if not quite handsome, to have cut a swath through the beauties of his generation.

She preferred not to be one of them.

Night before last, at the masked ball, Harold hadn't bothered getting down on one knee. He'd phrased his marriage proposal in terms that suggested he thought her answer, her *positive* answer, was a foregone conclusion. She'd been whisked away by a dance partner before she could respond. She'd kept her distance the rest of the evening, or as much of the evening as she could remember. She still had no idea how she'd ended up in her hotel room.

Who had drugged her? Who had taken her back to her hotel room? And why had he only stolen the Ghost, when he could have taken from her something very much more precious?

Fortunately, her dignity had remained intact, even if her trust in mankind had been shattered. Oh, how she wished she could love Harold! It would have made everything so much easier.

The earl was courting her with her father's permission and approval. She'd simply gone along for the ride, never dreaming that Harold would push so soon for an engagement, let alone marriage. She'd learned too late that Harold was more than ready to settle down. He'd been working in his father's import-export business for the past fifteen years, which made him what seemed to her a very ancient thirty-eight.

Lydia wasn't in love with the earl, but she'd continued dating him because she'd wanted to please her father. She'd kept hoping she would fall in love with him. It hadn't happened. In fact, she liked Harold less the more she got to know him.

To her horror, she heard the shower start running in the bathroom. She wondered when it would dawn on Harold that she couldn't be in the shower if she was standing here in front of him. She wondered what Harold would do if he knew another man was in her hotel bedroom.

Surprisingly, her mother hadn't approved of Harold Delaford as a prospective spouse. In fact, the Duchess had warned her to avoid all contact with him. When pressed, her mother had refused to give Lydia a reason for her dislike of the earl. In the end, it had been easier to date him to please her father than to avoid him to please her mother.

Her parents, Bella and Bull, were strange creatures to have ended up together. Her father was a larger-than-life character. An American by birth, he was the younger brother of Foster Benedict, an advisor to the American president. Bull had increased his father's banking fortune until he was one of the richest men in America.

Her mother, Bella, was the Duchess of Blackthorne, a title she held by virtue of the heroism, and subsequent death, of all her male forebears in World War II. In order to keep the Blackthorne title from being extinguished, Parliament had declared the dukedom could pass in either the male or the *female* line.

As the elder of twin girls, Isabella Wharton had become the Duchess of Blackthorne at birth. She would hold the title until her death, when Lydia's eldest brother, Oliver, currently Earl of Courtland, would become duke.

Lydia had always thought her parents' love story was romantic. Twenty-nine-year-old Bull had been dating Bella's second cousin when he'd met Bella at an embassy party in Washington, D.C. He'd fallen for seventeen-year-old Bella, and that had been the end of that. Bella and Bull were married a month later. Oliver had been born eight months after that.

A shadow crossed Lydia's mind. Rumors persisted that Oliver wasn't her father's son, that Bella had forced her father into marriage to give some other man's baby a name. Over the years, Oliver, the future Duke of Blackthorne, had been called bastard, and worse. It was a label difficult to deny, because her brown-eyed eldest brother had two blue-eyed parents.

Lydia had always thought it terribly unfair for Oliver to be punished for something that couldn't possibly be his fault. Maybe that was why he was her favorite brother.

She wondered if her father had known the truth when he married her mother. Regardless of whether Bull had been forced to marry Bella, their marriage had become a love match, and they'd been happy together for twenty-five years. The past ten were another story entirely.

Despite her parents' flaws, or perhaps because of them, she loved them desperately. Because her father was the most absent parent, she yearned for his approval. She wanted his love. She'd settle for having him *notice* her. Which was how she'd ended up with this unfortunate proposal from the Earl of Sumpter.

She found Harold's appearance at her hotel suite annoying. With four older brothers, she was used to male bravado. She might even have found his visit amusing, if it hadn't been for the man in the next room. She realized the shower was no longer running.

The earl grasped her hand and said, "Lydia, darling, will you marry me?"

She'd opened her mouth to respond when a brusque male voice demanded, "Tell me, honey, where the hell are my clothes?"

CHAPTER 6

*T*he earl jumped to his feet and glared with narrowed eyes at the half-naked man. He turned to her and demanded, "What the bloody hell is he doing here?"

Lydia's heart jumped to her throat as her gaze shot to the American who'd been sleeping in her bed.

Joe Warren stood stark naked except for a white towel wrapped low around his hips, his hair dripping in wet strands on forehead and nape. He leaned back against the door frame, cocked a brow, and waited.

Lydia stared at the triangle of dark curls on his broad chest. She was surprised to see that the jagged scar on his face continued down his body. It angled its way from his collar bone—across spectacular abs—all the way to his navel, disappearing under the edge of the towel. Once upon a time this warrior must have been bronzed and buff, but his deep tan had faded, and Lydia could see his ribs. His dark eyes met hers, then moved to the other man in the room.

Harold turned red in the face and glowered at Lydia. "Why do you have a half-naked man in your room?"

Lydia's temper sparked at the earl's presumption that he had any right to direct or control her behavior. "I don't owe you an explanation."

"I'm your fiancé," Harold blustered.

"No, Harold, you're not."

The earl backed up a step. He looked shocked.

Lydia reached out to touch his arm, but he jerked away.

"I'm sorry, Harold. I should have told you when you asked the first time. I can't marry you. I don't love you."

"What does that have to do with anything?" he retorted.

It was Lydia's turn to look shocked, although she knew she shouldn't be. For centuries aristocrats had used marriages for alliances to secure kingdoms, to consolidate property, to continue dynasties. There was nothing so different about Harold's proposal. It would unite two prosperous, upper-class British families. The beautiful daughter of a duchess was an appropriate wife for a wealthy earl who would someday be a marquess of the realm.

"My clothes?" Joe said into the silence.

"Oh. I—" Lydia heard a knock on the hotel room door and hoped it was the delivery she was expecting. She turned her back on both men and headed for the door. When she opened it she found a porter waiting with a valet cart stacked high with packages bearing designer labels. "Come in," she said, smiling at the porter. "Please take everything to the bedroom."

"What's all this?" Harold said as the porter pushed past him.

"Clothes for Joe." Lydia flushed when she realized how that must sound to the earl. "Joe doesn't have—" She cut herself off. Whatever explanation she made would reveal far too much about her desperate circumstances. She put her hands on her hips, looked her would-be fiancé in the eye, and said, "You should leave, Harold."

Harold stared daggers at Joe Warren, who'd stepped aside to allow the porter to push his load of packages into the only bedroom in the suite.

"Who the hell *are* you?" the earl asked in a crisp British voice.

"Who the hell are *you*?" Joe replied in his Texas drawl.

The earl bristled and turned his agitated gaze toward Lydia. "I want an explanation. What is a cur like this doing in your—"

"This isn't what you think," Lydia interrupted.

"Then what is it?"

"I can't tell you that."

The earl lifted an aristocratic brow. "Can't? Or won't?"

"It's the same thing," Lydia said.

"We'll see what your father has to say about this," Harold threatened.

"What I do is none of Daddy's business, either."

"You think not?"

"Harold—" Lydia bit her lip. She wasn't going to beg him to hold his tongue. She knew her father hated a tattletale. Maybe Harold would blacken himself so much in Bull's eyes that her father would decide that the earl wasn't such a perfect suitor after all.

Harold started toward the door, then turned on his heel and crossed back to Joe. He stopped short, perhaps alarmed by a subtle change, a sudden threatening awareness, in Joe's posture, and said through gritted teeth, "Keep your filthy hands off. She's mine."

Joe held his palms out to look at them, turned them over, and surveyed his knuckles. Obviously, right out of the shower, they were clean. He bunched his hands into fists as he met the earl's gaze. Then he turned to Lydia, as though the earl was of no account, and said, "Give me a hint, honey. Where the hell are my clothes?"

Lydia was appalled. This stranger was throwing gasoline on a raging fire, with no concern for who might get burned in the conflagration. Harold was a powerful man with international connections in banking and politics. He could make life very difficult for someone like American PI Joe Warren.

She looked again and realized it was Harold who seemed to be in the greater immediate danger.

Unshaven, wearing barely a stitch of clothing and with no weapon except his fists, the American looked like a feral beast poised to attack.

Harold must have sensed the same menace Lydia perceived, because he suddenly backed up a step.

The American didn't move so much as a hair.

Harold backed up another step and turned to Lydia. "I'll be in touch after I speak to your father." Then he turned and strode from the room.

The earl was followed almost immediately by the porter with his empty valet cart. Lydia grabbed some euros from an end table and put them in the porter's hand as he crossed her path, then locked the hotel door behind him. She resisted the urge to sigh with relief. Instead, she crossed back to the private investigator she'd hired to help her find the Ghost and said, "Was that really necessary? Provoking Harold like that?"

"It got him to leave, didn't it?"

Lydia shook her head. There was no reasoning with a Neanderthal. "Get dressed so we can go to work."

He glanced over his shoulder into the bedroom. "What is all that stuff?"

"A decent wardrobe. I can't be seen with you wearing that outfit you had on when you stepped off the plane."

"Where are my clothes?"

She sighed. She had to give him points for persistence. "They should be somewhere in there. I had them laundered and pressed. But I hope you won't decide to wear them. It's going to be hard enough for me not to be noticed running around Rome asking questions about a missing jewel. I'd rather not do it with a man dressed in military camouflage."

He rubbed the whiskers on his chin. "You have a point."

"You might want to shave. You'll find both an electric razor and a straight razor in the items that were just delivered. I hope everything fits. I told the concierge what I wanted and he did the shopping."

"I don't take charity."

"Fine. I'll send a bill to your firm."

The twist of his lips told her exactly what he thought of her efforts to have him dress like a normal human being. But she wasn't feeling particularly sensitive to anyone else's feelings right now. "For heaven's sake! They're just clothes."

He took a step back and closed the bedroom door in her face.

Lydia glared at the door, wondering what Joe Warren would be wearing when he came back out.

CHAPTER 7

*J*oe turned and stared at the packages the porter had stacked on the settee at the foot of the bed. He read the labels and found Gucci, Hermès, Brooks Brothers, Ralph Lauren, Canali, Prada, Brioni, even Cartier and Rolex. He began opening boxes, pulling out the contents and throwing them onto the unmade bed.

It didn't take long to realize nothing was off-the-shelf.

Everything had been custom-made, two white and two blue high-thread-count shirts, gold cuff links, gray and khaki trousers, a perfectly tailored blazer, a cashmere V-neck sweater, and silk ties in every color of the rainbow. Even the Italian leather shoes, pairs in both black and brown, seemed to be made especially for him.

Joe wondered how Miss High-and-Mighty had known what sizes to buy. She must have told the concierge to use the measurements from the clothing he'd worn when he'd arrived. Shirt, undershirt, shorts, trousers, socks, and shoes had all been missing when he'd woken up.

He had an image of himself looking as suave as the suitor who'd just left and snickered. You couldn't make a silk purse out of a sow's ear. He'd never be officer material, and he was proud of it. He'd been an army grunt, a sergeant who worked in the trenches, a man whose strength and reflexes and intelligence in battle had saved his own and other soldiers' lives. Clothes did *not* make the man. He would look ridiculous in these fashionable rags.

But he needed clean underwear and socks, and he didn't feel like hunting down his own stuff in all this mess. So he slipped on a pair of the white cotton shorts she'd provided.

Joe grinned. What the hell were these things made of? They felt a lot more like silk than a sow's ear. He reached for a white shirt and found it even softer than the shorts, if that was possible. He unfolded and unbuttoned the shirt and slid his arms into it and pulled it up over his shoulders. It felt like heaven against his skin.

He frowned at the shirt cuffs, which had no buttons. He drew the line at wearing cuff links. Instead, he folded the cuffs up to expose his forearms.

He let himself be tempted by the pair of gray slacks. The waist was a little big, but after the past six months of drinking his dinners, so was the waist on his cammie trousers. He looked for a belt and found a sleek, supple black leather belt with a modest silver buckle. He searched for a pair of black socks, found them, and experienced another sensory delight when he pulled them on. He threw the black-tasseled, loafer-type shoes, with their braided-leather tops, onto the floor and slipped his feet into them one at a time.

Perfect fit.

Joe walked around on the plush carpet, marveling at how the leather molded to his feet. He eyed the beautiful silk ties, but he wasn't comfortable with a tie around his neck, since most of his military life he'd gone without one. Instead, he picked up the navy-blue, cashmere V-necked sweater. It was soft as a baby's butt. He'd never owned, or wanted to own, anything made of cashmere, but he realized he might have been missing the boat. It felt good next to his skin.

He pulled the cashmere over his head and adjusted the shirt collar and refolded the shirt sleeves so they ended up outside the sweater, which he pulled halfway up his forearms. He limped over to look at himself in the mirror. He should have shaved, if he was going to, before he'd dressed. He had a three-day-old beard, which darkened his cheeks and chin. Hell. If he could live with the fancy clothes, she could live with the beard.

He realized he was hungry. And thirsty. He desperately needed a hair of the dog. Or maybe some aspirin. He recognized the pain in his temples as a hangover headache. He remembered Samantha's last words as she'd put him on the plane.

"You need to be sober to do this job, Joe."

Maybe he'd take advantage of the change of scenery, and the work, as an opportunity to dry out. It had been a long six months since the army had given him his walking papers.

His mouth felt sour. He remembered seeing shaving gear in the stuff the valet had brought, and sure enough, it was there, along with a comb, a toothbrush, mouthwash, and toothpaste. He gave his teeth a quick brush, gargled with some mouthwash, ran the comb through his hair, and wished again for a couple of aspirin. He took a quick look through the kit, but all he found was an expensive cologne.

He opened it and sniffed. Nice. But he didn't put it on. Bad enough to look like a gigolo without smelling like one.

Now that he was dressed, he might as well see if Miss High-and-Mighty wanted to get some chow. And a beer, of course. He opened the door and found her waiting for him.

She was seated on the couch, legs crossed at the ankle, wearing a sleeveless, square-necked black dress. It was something a lady might wear, not too short, not too tight, not too low-cut. Nevertheless, it managed to make him aware of her very female shape. He was pretty sure it wouldn't take much effort to get it off of her.

Forget what you're thinking, Joe. Don't start imagining what it might be like to see that dress come off her shoulders. Don't let yourself drown in those violet eyes. Stop looking. Now.

That wasn't as easy as it sounded.

Her hair was pinned up somehow so it was off her shoulders and away from her face, and he could see diamond studs in her ears. It was hard not to notice her gold-and-diamond watch and the pin on her dress sparkling with a multitude of jewels. She looked as wealthy as he knew she was.

He'd thought he looked pretty good, but he could see right away she looked disappointed.

"You didn't shave!"

He shrugged. "So what?"

She took a long, careful look at him, and he felt his body respond to the visual caress. Then she rose, a languid movement full of grace that made him wonder how it would feel to have her slide her sinuous body against his.

Keep your mitts, off, Joe, he warned himself. *She knows who she is and what she wants, and it isn't the likes of you. Don't even look, because you're likely to lose a hand, never mind your heart, if you try to touch.*

Her gaze roamed his body again from head to foot. "I wondered if everything would fit."

"Fits fine." Certain parts were fitting less well, the more she looked at him with those smoky violet eyes.

"Are they really okay?"

They were more than okay. He felt like a million bucks, which was probably about what this get-up cost. But he wasn't going to admit that to her. She already had him feeling off-kilter. He wasn't used to playing the supplicant with women. He was here to do a job for his sister, and he'd better remember it.

"Are we going to stand here jawing all day?" he said tersely. "I thought you wanted to find that necklace."

"I do," she replied. "First, I bought something else for you on my own, something I hope you'll like." She looked at him anxiously before she picked up a box from the coffee table and extended it to him.

"What is it?"

"Open it."

He took the box, which was oblong, narrow, and flat. It could have been filled with flowers. It wasn't.

He scowled as he pulled out a wooden cane. It was simple and beautiful, made of light oak with a gnarled wooden handle. He threw it back into the box and dropped the box on the table. "I don't need that."

She unexpectedly shoved him hard in the stomach.

He lost his balance and fell back on the arm of the couch.

She looked at him down her pert nose and said, "Yes, you do."

Joe hated her for speaking the truth. But the fact that he needed a cane didn't mean he had to use one. "I'm not using that thing."

"Suit yourself." She headed for the door but glanced back over her shoulder. "Just don't plan to lean on me when you're about to fall on your face."

Joe eyed the cane with malice. The elegant cane was one more piece of the ridiculous costume she'd conned him into wearing. But he'd never used a cane, and he wasn't going to start now. Furthermore, when he was gone from here—and he would be, as soon as Samantha found that damned missing Ghost—he would chuck this fancy gear faster than you could say "Dallas Cowboys."

"I need some chow," he said as he crossed to join her at the door. He waited for her to comment on his appearance in the clothes she'd bought. One word out of her and he was going to strip out of these fancy duds and put on his cammies and to hell with how he looked.

It seemed she knew men better than he knew women. Because all she said was, "Supper sounds wonderful. I'm starved. Where would you like to eat?"

"The hotel is fine with me," he replied.

"They serve wonderful pasta dishes in the garden restaurant."

"I'll settle for a blood-rare steak."

She looked annoyed for a moment. If Joe hadn't been watching her face he would have missed the expression. He realized she was used to hiding her feelings and wondered why she'd needed to perfect that sort of skill. When she didn't speak he said, "Something wrong?"

"It's too early to dine on steak at the hotel. Nothing's open yet."

He glanced at his watch. It was not quite six in the evening. When he looked up again, he saw a pained expression on her face.

She frowned at his watch. "Didn't you see the watch I bought?"

His face froze. It was one thing to wear a bunch of clothes she'd purchased for him. It was quite another to accept an expensive watch. He'd coveted the Rolex Mariner, all right, but he'd left it sitting in the box. "The watch I'm wearing keeps perfect time." He'd run many a mission wearing this watch. But she was right about one thing. The worn leather and scratched dial didn't go with the cashmere sweater and tasseled loafers. Neither did he, for that matter.

He waited for her to point that out. But she didn't.

"A paragon of tact," he muttered.

"What did you say?"

"Pasta's fine."

She led him to The Palm, a garden restaurant featuring wrought-iron tables and chairs bordered by ancient stone walls covered with ivy, and with an amazing view of the Borghese Gardens.

Lydia must have eaten at the restaurant a lot, because the waiter immediately brought a bottle of wine to the table along with a couple of glasses.

"Thank you, Armando," she said with a smile that Joe thought would have had anyone who was on the other end of it doing whatever she wanted. She turned to Joe, that killer smile still on her face. "Is wine all right with you?"

He was ready to agree, just to please her, but he didn't really like wine. He'd grown up on beer and whiskey, and that was what he preferred. "I'll take a beer," he told the waiter. "Whatever you've got."

The waiter named half a dozen European beers. Joe chose Heineken, the one brand he recognized.

"Very good choice," the waiter said. "Will you be dining?"

"Yes," Lydia said. "Would you bring us menus, please, Armando?"

Joe ordered spaghetti and meatballs, while Lydia chose a chicken salad. While they were waiting for their food to arrive, Joe's phone rang. He saw it was his sister and said, "I've got to take this." He turned his back on Lydia and asked, "What's the word?"

"Who is it?" Lydia asked anxiously. "Is there news about the Ghost?"

Joe held up a hand to silence her. "Uh-huh. I'll call you when we get there." He glanced at his watch. "We've just ordered supper. We'll head over there as soon as we're done."

When he ended the call Lydia asked, "Who was that?"

Joe started to say, "My sister." Instead he said, "My assistant in Texas. Someone sent an Internet message about the theft of the Ghost from the business office at the Westin Excelsior Hotel on Via Vittorio Veneto. Since no one except you and the thief knows the Ghost is missing, the presumption is that the thief sent the email."

She stood abruptly and set her napkin on the table. "We should go now. We can eat later."

"The email was sent early this morning. The thief is either still checked into the hotel or long gone. In either case, getting there in ten minutes, or an hour and ten minutes, isn't going to make a difference."

She hesitantly sat back down. "You sound very sure of yourself."

He shrugged. "If I were the thief, I'd be long gone from Rome by now."

"Do you think he'll try to sell the Ghost?"

"What makes you think the thief was a man?" Joe asked.

"I didn't spend time with any women I didn't know at the masked ball, which is where I'm sure the thief singled me out," she said. "The women I know wouldn't need to steal if they wanted a jewel like the Ghost. They'd buy it, or have their husbands or boyfriends buy it for them."

He frowned. "I can't believe you 'borrowed' something so valuable, and irreplaceable, without asking. What were you thinking?"

To give her credit, she looked guilty. Then her chin came up and she said, "Oliver arranged for me to keep the Ghost for ten days, which means we have time to find it before it's missed. Once we get it back, I'll confess what I've done and take whatever punishment Mother metes out."

"And if we don't get it back?"

"That isn't an option." She laid a delicate hand on his bare forearm. "Emily, my mother's assistant, says you're the best." She looked deep into his eyes. "I'm relying on you, Joe."

He held his arm still, afraid that if he moved, Lydia would notice what she was doing and move her hand away like a frightened wild thing. He felt a little dizzy looking into those deep purple pools. He was falling hard, and he didn't give a damn. All he knew was that she needed him. He was willing to go to hell and back if that's what it took to help her.

Joe just hoped his sister could figure out how to find that damned missing necklace, because he didn't have the first clue where to look for the Ghost.

CHAPTER 8

*B*ull Benedict stared out the window of the Paris office of his banking empire toward the Eiffel Tower, wondering where his wife was right now. He spent a lot of time wondering about Bella. Too much, considering how the Duchess had betrayed him. When he'd seen her two weeks ago, on Mother's Day, at the Benedict family mansion in Virginia, Bella had seemed subdued. The fact that she'd ended up in the emergency room of a cardiac hospital in Richmond later the same day had scared him shitless. What if she'd died?

She claimed she'd merely had a panic attack. But the woman he loved had nerves of steel. Bella never gave an inch, never backed away, never revealed a weakness, assuming one even existed.

Bull stopped himself right there. Loving Bella had only meant pain over the past ten years. The twenty-five years before that had been a hell-raising, hair-raising, wild and woolly ride full of joy. He wouldn't have missed a moment of their life together, even knowing how it had ended.

If only it had *ended,* he thought. This *thing* between them would never end. He'd felt Bella's power over him as recently as two weeks ago. He'd taken one look at her and felt on fire for her. He'd wanted to lick her skin, to thrust himself inside her, to sieve his hands into her silky black hair and hold her close as he kissed her senseless.

But they hadn't even kissed in greeting. The distance between them, after ten years of marital separation, seemed insurmountable. And yet, Bull wanted that closeness back again.

It was his fault they'd separated in the first place. He hadn't given her a chance to explain what he'd seen. He'd taken one look at his naked wife and her lover in his own marital bed and bolted, afraid he would kill them both if he got anywhere near the sheets where Bella lay entwined with another man.

It was three days before he'd returned to confront her. Even then, when she'd begged him to listen, he'd refused. He'd been a wounded animal, unable to express the pain that made him want to tear out his aching heart.

"There's an explanation for what you saw," she claimed.

"Was it him?" he shot back. "Was it Oliver's father?"

She'd looked stricken and remained mute, and he'd had his answer.

He'd forgiven her for marrying him when she was carrying the child of another man, because by the time he knew of it, he was deeply in love with her. But there was no forgiveness in him for taking another man, the *same* man, into their bed after twenty-five years of marriage. She'd broken the promise she'd made that she would never betray him again.

He'd been a tortured soul ever since, wondering who that unforgettable mystery man was. He'd never asked the son of a bitch's name, and Bella had never offered it.

Bull thought back to the first time he'd seen Bella, at a British Embassy reception in Washington, D.C. His heart had leapt in his chest when she'd smiled up at him and asked, "Are you really called Bull?"

His mouth was suddenly bone dry, and he'd needed to clear his throat before he could say, "I am."

"Then you're the one courting my cousin."

Bull had come to the reception with twenty-one-year-old Lady Regina Delaford, daughter of the British ambassador to the United States, the Marquess of Tenby. He'd dated the girl exactly twice, which wasn't even close to "courting" as far as he was concerned. Instead of denying the relationship he said, "Your cousin?"

"Second cousin, very far removed," she explained, her smile becoming a mischievous grin. "I'm Isabella Wharton. You may call me Bella."

She said it as though she were the Queen of England allowing him the honor of addressing her, Bull thought. Before he could say a word, Regina showed up at his elbow, slid her arm possessively through his, and said, "You're looking very fine tonight, Bella."

"You didn't tell me he was so handsome," Bella said to her cousin.

Bull had flushed at the discussion of his looks.

"He's mine, Bella, so don't get any ideas," Regina said.

He'd eyed Regina sideways but didn't contradict her. He would tell her later, in private, that she didn't own him.

"Surely you won't mind sharing him long enough for us to have a dance," Bella said, taking Bull's hand and leading him away from her cousin onto the dance floor.

He'd marveled at her audacity, but he was entranced by her violet eyes, her perfect alabaster skin, and her dark, shiny hair. Full breasts were revealed by a hint of teasing cleavage in a full-length, strapless black dress that fit her like a snake's skin. She smelled of some dusky perfume that made him think of black silk sheets on a large bed. He was glad for the chance to hold her in his arms.

She kept a bare inch between them, enough for him to feel the heat of her body but not the contours of it. He wanted her closer and pressed his hand against the small of her back until their bodies touched from breast to hip.

He heard a small gasp, and when she met his gaze he saw that her violet eyes had darkened until they looked like dangerous storm clouds. She caught her lower lip in her teeth as she lowered her lids to hide her eyes from him. "I wish you were mine," she said in a voice that sent shivers down his spine.

His breath caught in his throat. Was she saying what it

seemed she was saying? "Look at me, Bella."

Her lashes came up, and when their eyes met, he felt his body harden to stone. She was Eve, the first woman, seemingly innocent but tempting him to sin.

Bull stopped dancing, grabbed her hand, and said, "Come with me." He didn't give her a chance to refuse, simply headed for the staircase that led to the upper rooms in the embassy.

"My aunt will be looking for me," she protested. "Where are you taking me?"

He found an empty room intended for meetings, with a long conference table surrounded by rolling chairs, pulled her inside, and closed and locked the door.

He pressed her against the door with his hips and caught a handful of her hair before he lowered his mouth to hers. God help him, she tasted sweet! He sought the zipper along the back of her dress and slid it down.

She made a sound of protest that was lost as he deepened the kiss. Her hands slid from his shoulders up into his hair and then back down to his nape, making him quiver with desire.

As the sleek black dress slid into a pool on the floor he released her to see what he had. She stepped out of the circle of material and eased her feet from her high heels, lowering her three inches, so her head came to the middle of his chest.

Her breasts were high and full in a black strapless bra, her waist easily spanned by his hands, her stomach flat. Her long, slender legs were encased, heaven help him, in black silk stockings held by a beribboned black garter belt over a scrap of black underwear.

He released the bra and her warm breasts fell into his hands. He lowered his mouth and heard her gasp as he sucked a nipple into his mouth. His fingers and thumb teased the other nipple before his mouth gave it equal attention.

She moaned, and his body tautened.

He looked into her eyes and whispered, "Touch me."

She leaned back with dazed eyes to look at him, and he saw her cheeks were flushed. "I . . ."

He took her hand and pressed it against the fly of his tuxedo trousers where his body waited, hard and ready. He closed his eyes and held his breath as she slowly, with a sound of female appreciation, traced the length of him.

"I want you." His voice sounded strange in his ears.

She didn't respond in words, merely reached up and shoved his tuxedo jacket off his shoulders, all the while looking into his eyes. She reached up to release the bow tie at his throat, smiling like a cat with a pot of cream as she pulled it free. When he reached for the top button on his shirt, she stopped his hand. "I want to do it."

She took her time, and his heart was pounding by the time he'd been relieved of suspenders, shirt, and cummerbund. Her hands played in the dark hair that covered his chest. She leaned forward to tease one of his nipples with her teeth, and he drew in a sharp breath.

She looked up at him with those amazing violet eyes and asked, "Did I hurt you?"

Everything that happened afterward occurred without conscious thought. Patience gone, he reached out and ripped away the fragile silk between her legs, then freed himself and lifted her enough to thrust himself deep inside.

She was warm and wet, and when she set her fingertips at his nape and stroked, he came so hard and fast and long that a guttural sound of agony was wrenched from his throat.

He dropped his head against her shoulder, panting, ashamed at how quickly he'd come. He hadn't left a woman so unsatisfied since he was fourteen and didn't know any better.

He lifted his head to apologize, took one look at the sated violet eyes staring back at him, and smiled as he placed a tender kiss beneath her ear.

He felt her shiver and was ready to play some more when Bella surprised him by saying he should go and that she would stay and repair herself. He'd taken a second look at her face and seen something in her eyes that bothered him. Fear? Guilt? Shame?

He hadn't stayed to ask, because she clearly wanted him gone. He'd left knowing that he had to spend more time with her, to see if what had happened between them would happen again or whether it had simply been a time out of time.

When he'd called the next day to ask Bella to share dinner and the ballet, she'd refused, citing his relationship with her second cousin and adding, "What happened shouldn't have happened."

Bull didn't ask again. He'd never begged a woman for

anything, and he wasn't about to start. But there had been an ache inside, as though a hole had been torn in his heart.

A month later, the girl's aunt had come to him and said Bella was pregnant, that he was the father, and that he would have to marry her.

Bull had laughed in her face. He had no intention of marrying at twenty-nine. Then the old witch had dropped her bomb. Bella was only seventeen. If Bull didn't marry her, he would be charged with statutory rape.

Bull had stopped laughing. He was rich enough to hire lawyers to drag out whatever charges there were against him for years. But a man in a conservative business like banking couldn't afford to smirch his reputation. He'd agreed to marry Bella to give the child a name, but he'd vowed to make her pay for what she'd done to him.

Bull sighed. It was a marriage made in hell that had somehow found its way into the light and then descended into hell again.

There had been a nasty scene with Bella's furious cousin, Regina, after she told the tabloids that billionaire banker Bull Benedict had been blackmailed into marrying Isabella Wharton, Duchess of Blackthorne. Bull had made it clear that nothing and no one on earth could have compelled him to marry Bella if he hadn't been enchanted by her.

It wasn't until his brown-eyed son was born—a biological impossibility considering his blue eyes and Bella's violet ones— that Bull realized how badly he'd been duped. But by then he was head over heels in love with his wife. He'd confronted Bella, and she'd admitted that there had been someone before him, but she'd sworn that she hadn't known whose child she was carrying when she married him.

"So you picked the richest goose to pluck," he'd snarled.

"My aunt did that," she'd replied bitterly.

It turned out that the Blackthorne estate in England, Blackthorne Abbey, was in ruins and needed an infusion of capital. Bella's aunt had taken advantage of Bella's "misfortunate accident" to trap her a wealthy husband.

Bull hadn't wanted to know who'd fathered his eldest son. But he'd always wondered. He'd felt particularly betrayed by Bella's infidelity ten years ago when she wouldn't deny that the person in bed with her was the same man who'd sired Oliver. He should have waited until the man turned around so he could see his face, should have confronted him then and there instead of running like some scared rabbit.

Ten years later, Bull's face flamed anew with anger and humiliation. He made himself focus on the beautiful summer flowers his secretary had put on his desk and the blue sky studded with fluffy clouds and the spiraling architecture that made Paris a haven for artists, as he waited for his heart rate to slow. He wished he'd acted differently. He wished he'd confronted Bella and her lover. At least then they might have been able to fight it out and either move forward or end their marriage.

Instead, they were stuck in this nightmarish limbo.

The jarring ring of his office phone was a welcome distraction from his troubling thoughts. Bull answered the phone as he always did, "Benedict."

"I have something you might want back," a distorted voice said.

"Who is this?" Bull demanded.

"Twenty-five million. That's my price . . ."

Bull's heart began racing as he imagined what someone might have stolen from him that was worth that much. *Bella.* He imagined her kidnapped, terrified and being held for ransom.

Before he could say he'd pay anything to have her back, the caller finished, "If you want the Ghost back."

"What?"

"Too much? Too bad. Pay or I'll sell it on the black market, and you'll never see it again."

Bull laughed. He knew Bella kept her jewels in a safe in the dungeon at Blackthorne Abbey. They were as tightly protected and inaccessible to thieves as the Crown Jewels. "If this is a joke, it's in bad taste."

"Check it out. The Ghost is a ghost." The caller laughed, a horrible sound, distorted as it was.

A moment later a picture appeared on Bull's phone of the Ghost lying on a copy of that morning's London *Times.*

Was this some kind of joke? He would have sworn Bella would never loan the necklace to anyone. But it clearly was not in the vault at Blackthorne Abbey.

"Presuming you do, in fact, have the Ghost," he said, "I'd need at least a week to get that much money in one place."

The caller remained silent for a few moments. "You have forty-eight hours. I'll be in touch."

Bull found himself listening to a dead phone. He laughed shakily. He could hardly believe someone had just called to ransom the Ghost. Of course, the Ghost was priceless, not just in monetary value, but for what it meant to him and Bella.

He could still remember the day he'd given it to her.

After she'd given him three more healthy sons, Bull hadn't wanted his wife to get pregnant again. She'd had a C-section with their youngest boy, and he didn't want her to have to go through that again. But Bella had wanted him to have a daughter.

She'd laughed at his fear and denied her own. "You need the experience of having your darling daughter wrap you around her little finger. And I want a little girl I can dress in pretty clothes."

He'd warned her that they would probably end up with another boy, but she'd been relentless, in the way only Bella could be. Teasing him. Taunting him. Refusing to bed him when he was using protection, meanwhile assuring him that she was willing and eager to make love to him as often and in as many positions as he could imagine, and in some he hadn't imagined yet, so long as he came to her naked and ready.

What red-blooded male could resist such an invitation?

Bull hadn't.

The delivery of their daughter had been as difficult as the doctors had warned it would be. Bella had barely survived the birth, but she'd given him the precious little girl she'd promised. Lydia Jane Benedict, a tiny copy of her mother, had promptly stolen his heart.

Bull had given Bella a gift of jewels on the birth of each of their sons, but he'd wanted something special to celebrate the birth of his one and only daughter. He couldn't believe the Ghost of Ali Pasha, an enormous teardrop pearl, was on the market, but he'd jumped at the chance to buy it, despite its unsavory reputation. He didn't believe a pearl could cause bad luck. He didn't believe in jewels being jinxed.

The one-of-a-kind teardrop pearl had once been owned by the Ali Pasha of Yannina, an Albanian pasha from the western part of Rumelia in the Ottoman Empire. The notoriously cruel pasha had roasted rebels, flayed a man alive, and killed another by having his bones broken with a sledgehammer. Beginning in 1788, Ali Pasha had ruled most of Albania, western Greece, and the Peloponnese for more than thirty years.

He gave the pearl as a gift to his favorite concubine, a Circassian woman named Juba. Shortly thereafter, Juba was poisoned by another concubine who was jealous. When the guilty party wouldn't reveal herself, Ali Pasha ordered every single one of the three hundred Christian, Muslim, Albanian, and Circassian women in his harem executed.

When Ali Pasha was finally defeated by his enemies and beheaded, he was wearing Juba's pearl. His head was sent to the Sultan Mahmud II, where it was presented on a silver plate, the pearl still around the pasha's throat. The sultan took the pearl as a prize of war—and was strangled by it in his bed.

Thus began the legend that the teardrop pearl possessed the ghost of Ali Pasha, which had wreaked a terrible vengeance on his enemy.

The Ghost of Ali Pasha ended up as part of the Spanish royal jewels. King Ferdinand VII was pictured wearing the pearl in 1806 in a painting by Goya, just before he was forced to abdicate the throne in favor of the Emperor Napoleon. The king hadn't lost his head while he owned the Ghost, but he'd lost his position as head of state.

In 1840 Queen Isabella II of Spain gave the Ghost to Queen Victoria of England as a wedding present. The British queen feared the legend that went along with the pearl and sent it as a gift to Frederick II when he became King of Prussia. The king died without ever having children, keeping the legend alive. The Ghost somehow found its way to France and was sold to Tiffany's in the late 19th century at an auction of French royal jewels.

Bull had arranged to have the enormous, perfect teardrop pearl set in a necklace with all the other precious and semi-precious stones he'd given to his wife over the years—sapphires, emeralds, rubies, and diamonds. The result was stunning. And priceless.

The Ghost had a value for insurance purposes, of course, of twenty-five million. But he wouldn't have sold it for twice that, because every time he saw it around his wife's throat, it reminded me of the night they had made love and created their daughter. The day Bull gave Bella the Ghost was a happy day, maybe the happiest day, in his life. And the beginning of the end of their happiness as a couple.

The Ghost was cursed, all right.

Bull wondered if the Ghost had really been stolen, or if someone was trying to fleece him. He was a man of action, but he was also a very careful man. Rather than go off half-cocked, he called Smythe, the butler at Blackthorne Abbey, who had the keys to everything, including the vault in the dungeon.

"Smythe," the butler said when he answered the call. "How may I assist you, sir."

Bull smiled. Smythe was the most recent in a long line of Smythe butlers to the Blackthorne family, going back several centuries. The butler was always reserved but always capable of providing whatever service was required.

"I need you to check the vault and see if the Ghost is still there," Bull said.

"I don't need to look, sir, to tell you the Ghost isn't there."

Bull was startled by the butler's response. "Where is it?"

"On instructions from Courtland, I had the Ghost delivered to Lady Lydia in Rome. I expect it to be returned shortly. Is there a problem?"

"No. Thank you, Smythe." Bull ended the call. He pinched the bridge of his nose as he considered the possibilities in light of what he now knew. Did Lydia ever receive the Ghost? Was it stolen in transit? Did Oliver have it? Did he know where it was? Why did Oliver make the request to send the Ghost to Lydia and not Bella? Did Bella know the Ghost was missing?

The best way to get answers was to go directly to the source. He clicked on the number to call his daughter's cell phone. She picked up on the fourth ring.

"Hello, Daddy."

Just the sound of his daughter's voice made him feel warm inside. It had been too long since he'd seen Lydia. He should try harder to spend time with his children, although that was difficult with the rift between him and his wife, since it meant the kids had to visit her in one place and him in another. Not to mention how difficult it was to get five grown children, with completely different lives, together in one place.

Bull forced himself to focus on the issue at hand. "I got a strange phone call this morning."

"I couldn't accept Harold's proposal. I'm sorry if that upsets you, Daddy, but I just don't love him."

Bull was taken aback. He'd thought Harold Delaford would be a calming influence on his flighty daughter, but he'd had no idea their courtship had progressed so far. "That isn't why I called."

"It isn't? Then why are you calling? Is mother all right?"

"Your mother's fine."

"And Oliver and Payne and Riley and Max?"

"They're fine, too, so far as I know. I called about the Ghost." The silence on the other end of the line was a dead giveaway. "Do you have it?"

"Of course I have it. I borrowed it. Oliver arranged it."

"With your mother's permission?" Bull asked.

"I think he got her permission," Lydia said. "Does Mother want it back?"

She never gave him a chance to answer, just kept talking.

"Oliver said I could wear it to a charity event next week in Rome, for the publicity it will create and the money it will raise. I'd hate to go back on my promise. I'll make sure it gets back into the vault immediately afterward. I promise."

"You're sure you have it safe?"

"Why would you ask that?"

Bull debated whether to tell her about the call he'd received and decided there was no sense worrying her. Someone must have done some fancy photo-shopping and was trying to fleece him. Surely, if the Ghost was missing, Lydia would have admitted it and asked for his help.

"Just be careful," he said. "Be sure you have security with you when you're wearing the Ghost."

"I will, Daddy. I promise."

"I miss you, sweetheart."

"I miss you, too, Daddy."

Bull tried to think of an excuse to have her come see him in Paris but couldn't come up with one. Besides, he couldn't expect his children to drop what they were doing to come see him just because he was lonely. "Where are you keeping the Ghost?" he asked.

"In the safe at the Hotel Hassler. It might as well be in Fort Knox," she said with a laugh.

The laugh sounded forced, but maybe he was hearing things that weren't there. "Take care of yourself."

"Don't worry, Daddy. I'll be fine. There's someone at the door. I have to go."

"About Harold," he said.

"Oh, Daddy, please don't be angry with me. I can't help how I feel."

"I was going to say that whatever you decide is fine with me."

He heard a relieved sigh. "Thank you, Daddy. I love you."

Bull stared at his dead phone thoughtfully. Either the phone call demanding ransom for the Ghost was a hoax, or his daughter was lying through her teeth. In any event, Oliver didn't have the right to loan his mother's jewelry without her permission. He needed to speak with his eldest son.

Even as he thought the words, eldest son, Bull realized he thought of Oliver in exactly those terms. It didn't matter that Oliver didn't share his blood, he loved him as fiercely as any of his other children. However, he wasn't sure Oliver felt the same way towards him. Despite his efforts, there had always been a moat between the two of them that Oliver seemed reluctant to cross.

Bull made the call to Oliver's cell phone, but there was no answer. When he heard Oliver's voice asking him to leave a message, he wondered if his son had recognized his caller ID and refused to answer, or whether he really wasn't there.

Instead of leaving a phone message he texted: "Did you loan the Ghost to Lydia? Call me."

Bull pursed his lips. His text read like an accusation and an order. That was liable to put Oliver's back up and keep him from getting in touch. Not that he was liable to respond anyway. Oliver did what Oliver wanted to do when Oliver wanted to do it. His son was every bit as bullheaded as he was himself.

Bull realized the supposed theft of the Ghost gave him a valid excuse for contacting Bella. He picked up his phone again, then hesitated. Ever since their abortive meeting on Mother's Day at the Seasons, he'd realized he should have let her finish speaking that long-ago day, when he'd caught her with her lover, instead of cutting her off. If Bella needed to confess her sins in order for them to reconcile, then he needed to listen.

After the scare Bella had given him at the hospital, he'd thought a lot about how short and precious life was. He'd tried to find a woman to replace his wife, but every woman he compared to Bella came up short. He'd been in love with her since the first moment he laid eyes on her, and he'd love her till his dying day. If he could forgive—and forget—the past, perhaps there was a way for them to be happy together again.

He'd been too proud to take the first step toward peace. He was equally certain Bella never would.

But the years were taking their toll. The love between them

was slowly but surely being ground to dust, stuck between a rock and a hard place. It was time—past time—to move on, to reconcile or divorce. He wanted this awful life of pain to end.

Bull picked up the phone and called his wife.

CHAPTER 9

*O*liver read the text from his father and forcefully deleted it. He hadn't been in contact with his father for more than a year, and that was all Bull had to say? *Bloody hell! It's a pearl necklace. Irreplaceable, but not a matter of life and death. Why couldn't you just ask me how I am?*

He didn't owe Bull an explanation for anything he did, but especially not for loaning the Ghost to Lydia. His mother had given him control of the vault at Blackthorne Abbey, trusting him to use that power wisely. He always had. Or he thought he had. What was going on with the Ghost?

Oliver shivered. He was in Argentina, and it was the beginning of winter on the other side of the hemisphere from Paris. But it was the cold he felt on the inside, rather than the weather, that left him feeling chilled. He had to admit Bull Benedict had never treated him any differently than any of his biological children. But Oliver had known from a very early age that he wasn't like his siblings. It was his eyes, of course, that gave him away. They weren't just brown, they were such a dark brown that there was no way to hide the stain of his birth. Somewhere out there was a brown-eyed man who'd had sex with his violet-eyed mother, and then cut and run.

He knew his mother well enough to believe that if Bella had wanted to be married to the man who'd planted his seed, she would have made it happen. He'd heard the rumors about how Bull had been forced into marrying Bella because she was only seventeen when she'd gotten pregnant. But he knew Bull well enough to believe that if he hadn't wanted to marry Bella, he would have found a way out of it. It would have been simple, considering the fact that the child in Bella's womb didn't even have the same blood type as the man whose name was on Oliver's birth certificate.

Oliver had spent his entire life looking into the eyes of every man who said hello to his mother, wondering *Is he the one?* He'd thought for sure his biological father's identity would have come out ten years ago, when his mother had bedded her former paramour again. But Bella had separated from Bull rather than telling her husband the name of her lover.

It had taken Oliver a long time to make peace with the fact that he was probably never going to know who had sired him. Although *making peace* was not exactly how he'd dealt with the matter in boarding school. He'd fought anyone and everyone who'd suggested his mother was a whore and his father was a dupe. He'd made use of his sharp tongue to avoid fighting whenever possible. But he'd also gotten good with his fists. As he'd matured—he was taller and broader in the shoulders than any of his brothers—he'd found his size alone was often enough to keep mouths shut and fists in pockets.

Bull had wanted him to come into the banking business with him, but Oliver knew he'd die if he found himself caged in a glass-walled building. Bull had given each of his children—including Oliver—a substantial trust fund, so they could either choose a career or not work at all.

Oliver had suggested to his siblings that they form a foundation with their trust funds. They'd all agreed, and they met by Skype quarterly to discuss what good work the Castle Foundation was going to support. Each of them had a stipend from the foundation, but it wasn't enough to live the life of complete leisure they would have had if they'd kept their money for themselves. It had become necessary for each of them to find something to do with their lives.

Oliver had fallen into his occupation accidentally. A painting had been stolen from a museum that was supported by the Castle Foundation, and Oliver had begun investigating who might have taken it. The trail had led across several European countries and eventually two continents, and he'd found the chase exciting. Oliver hadn't bothered capturing the thief, he'd merely stolen back the painting and arranged for it to be replaced in the museum, with no one the wiser as to how it had been returned.

He liked the anonymity of his work, which gave him

the freedom to move about without his true objective being suspected. Lately he'd focused on items that were stolen during World War II. He had good resources for locating a missing item, but recovering the art or artifact and getting it back across borders to its original owner was often a serious challenge.

Right now he was on the trail of a Russian triptych that had disappeared from a Greek Orthodox church during the occupation of Stalingrad. Considering how badly that battle had gone for the Germans, whoever had taken it had to be somebody important enough to get out of the city before the Germans were finally forced to surrender.

Oliver had tracked down the son of a German general, whom he believed was the culprit. The young SS officer had been sent back to Germany from Stalingrad on a diplomatic mission around the time the triptych had gone missing and had fled to Argentina before the end of the war. He was now a very elderly man living with his elderly son in a walled hacienda outside Buenos Aires. Oliver had been scoping out the hacienda for the best way to retrieve the stolen artifact when he'd received the text from Bull.

Oliver realized he wasn't going to be able to concentrate on the job at hand until he'd satisfied his curiosity about why Bull had inquired about the Ghost.

He faded back into the pampas and phoned his sister. He realized it must be early evening in Rome and wondered if she was in some club where she couldn't hear her phone.

"Oliver! What a surprise!" Lydia said when she answered.

"Where's the Ghost, Lydia?"

Utter silence.

"Bull called me and asked if I'd loaned you the necklace. Why would he do that?"

"He called me, too," Lydia said breathlessly. "I have no idea why he's asking about the Ghost, Oliver. I told him I have it and it's fine. I wore it two nights ago, and I'm planning to wear it again next week."

Lydia had told him that she had their mother's permission to borrow the necklace, and he'd believed her. Now he wondered if she'd lied. He didn't know his youngest sister well, since he and his brothers had been at different boarding schools from her all their lives, but he'd given her the benefit of the doubt.

Had Bella come looking for the necklace, discovered it missing, and not known where it was? But that wouldn't explain why Bull had called, instead of Bella, asking about the Ghost.

Unless his mother used the missing necklace as an excuse to get in touch with his father.

"I presume you're taking good care of the necklace," he said.

"It's in the Hotel Hassler safe," she assured him. "Don't worry, Oliver. I'll be sure it's returned to the vault at Blackthorne Abbey right on schedule."

He heard a male voice in the background and asked, "Who's that with you?"

Silence again. And then, "I don't ask you about your love life, Oliver. I don't appreciate your asking about mine."

Oliver chuckled. "Watch out for fortune hunters."

"I don't have a fortune anymore," she said pertly. "I gave it to the Castle Foundation."

"Be careful, kid. The Duchess will have a fit if anything happens to that necklace."

"I'm always careful," she said. "Have you spoken to Mother lately?"

Oliver scowled. "I sent my regrets to her on Mother's Day. Other than that, no, I haven't been in touch. Why do you ask?"

Instead of answering his question, she said, "I've got to go, Oliver. Is there anything else?"

I miss you. I love you. Take care of yourself.

"That's all," he said. "Be good."

Lydia laughed. She'd been in more trouble in boarding school than all of the rest of them combined. "Goodbye, Oliver."

Oliver found himself listening to a dead phone. He tucked it back in his pocket as he tried to remember the most recent time he and his brothers and sister had all been together in one place. He had to go back a long way, to Christmas fifteen years ago. The last time they'd Skyped, he'd been in Argentina, Riley had been in Hong Kong, Payne had been in Greece, Max had been in London, and Lydia had been in Rome. Richmond, Virginia, was a long way for any of them to go in response to a summons from Bella. Which is why, he supposed, none of his siblings had made the trip.

There was a good reason, other than distance, why he hadn't gone. It was simply too painful to be anywhere near his mother when she was in so much pain from being estranged from Bull. The past ten years had been miserable ones for all of them. He wished his parents—the only parents he knew— would figure out a way to bury the hatchet, because their misery kept him and his siblings from gathering at Black-thorne Abbey for Christmas as they used to do.

The sad truth was, however much he felt separated by his birth when he was with his brothers and sister, he desperately missed spending time with them.

Oliver gritted his teeth so hard his jaw muscle flexed. He still had no idea why Bull had asked about the Ghost. Apparently, Bull had talked with Lydia, who'd reassured him she had the Ghost. There was no reason for him to contact Bull. But he was the only father Oliver had, and he owed him the courtesy—and the respect—of a response.

He texted: I had the Ghost sent to Lydia in Rome. She will return it to the vault at Blackthorne Abbey after she wears it to a charity event next week.

Then he disappeared into the tall grass.

CHAPTER 10

*E*mily held out the phone to Bella, who was resting in a lounge chair on a stone patio in Santorini, Greece, and said in a shocked voice, "It's your husband, Your Grace."

Bella stared at the phone without touching it. Despite all the wishing and hoping she'd done, Bull hadn't phoned her in ten years. He'd surprised her by showing up at the Seasons on Mother's Day, but his visit had been cut short when she'd had that episode with her heart that had landed her in the hospital in Richmond. *Panic attack*. Ha! The only panic she'd felt was terror that Bull would find out her secret. Bella put a fist against her chest, fighting for breath.

The truth was she was dying.

"Your Grace," Emily said with alarm. "Do you need oxygen?"

Bella forced herself to take several slow, deep breaths. "I'm all right, Emily." But her heart was racing.

After all this time, the most likely reason Bull had called was because something had happened to one of their children. Bella put a hand to her chest, to remind herself to stay calm, then took the phone with a trembling hand and said, "Hello, Bull."

Her voice came out raspy, sexy. She fought the knot in her throat as she asked, "Are the children all right?"

"As far as I know," Bull replied.

Bella heaved a relieved sigh. Her voice was still sharp with the fear she'd felt as she said, "Then why did you call?" Was he ready, at long last, to hear her explanation for what had happened ten years ago?

After a brief hesitation he said, "I'm calling about the Ghost."

That statement was so far from what Bella had hoped to hear that she was stunned into silence. She rose and walked to the edge of the patio overlooking the sea, so Emily wouldn't hear the disappointment in her voice as she asked, "What about it?"

"Did you loan it to Lydia?"

"No. Why do you ask?" *And why are you calling me to talk about a necklace when we have so many more important things to discuss. Like the separate lives we lead. Like whether we can ever find a way to forgive each other and be husband and wife again.*

"I'm asking because I got a strange call this morning from someone who disguised his—or her—voice asking me to pay a twenty-five million dollar ransom if I wanted the Ghost back."

Bella frowned. "That makes no sense. The Ghost is in the vault at Blackthorne Abbey."

"Let's take this one step at a time. First, did you loan the Ghost to Lydia."

"Of course not."

"I just spoke to her in Rome, and she claims to have it. She's wearing it to a charity event next week."

"How did she get it?"

"Apparently Oliver arranged to have it sent to her."

"He has access to the vault," Bella said. "And my complete trust."

"Then Lydia must have told him she had your permission to wear it."

"Surely not." Even as she spoke the words, Bella realized it was entirely possible Lydia had hedged the truth to acquire the necklace. "She must be frantic if it's been stolen from her," she murmured. "Especially since she never got my permission to borrow it."

"When I called Lydia to ask about the necklace, she swore that she had your permission to wear the Ghost, and that she was keeping it in the safe at the Hotel Hassler," Bull said. "We know that half that sentence was a lie. I'm wondering if she might have lost the Ghost—or had it stolen—and is afraid to admit what's happened."

Bella wasn't sure what to say. "Why did you call me, Bull?

This seems like a matter for the police."

"I thought you might want to help me find out the truth."

"I have a private investigator I can call—"

"No, Bella. I thought the two of us might do some investigating. Together."

Bella recognized the olive branch Bull was extending. It wasn't an apology, but it was an offer to spend time together, which might be a first step toward reconciliation. She was tempted to reach out and take it.

And ignore the elephant in the room? What about Bull's accusation that I cheated on him with Oliver's father? Should I pretend all is forgiven? Is all forgiven?

Bella doubted it. "Are you ready to talk about what happened ten years ago?"

There was no sound on the line for so long that Bella thought the connection had been lost.

At last Bull said, "Is that really necessary?"

So he was willing to let bygones be bygones. Which wasn't exactly the same thing as forgiving and forgetting.

She'd been wrongly accused and unjustly abandoned, and Bull saw no reason to apologize? Bella felt her adrenaline spiking as her anger rose. She struggled for breath, knowing that her heart was having trouble keeping up with the stress she was putting on it. In a few moments she wouldn't have enough breath to speak without revealing the debilitating condition she'd so successfully kept hidden from her family.

"I think Warren and Warren Investigations can handle the situation. They're very good at what they do."

"It's your necklace. Have them give me a call."

Was that regret she heard in his voice? Or was it resignation? "I will," Bella replied.

"And Bella . . ."

Bella waited hopefully for Bull to finish his sentence. Finally she asked, "Is there something else, Bull?"

"I miss you."

Bella felt her heart—her very fragile heart—squeeze. She opened her mouth to speak and closed it again. She'd missed him, too, more than she could bear. But she didn't respond in kind. She simply gasped, "I'll be in touch," and ended the call.

Bella swore under her breath, furious that, at fifty-four, her body was in such a fragile state. She'd injured herself in a skiing accident in the Alps three years ago, and the scar tissue on her heart had left her with only another year, or maybe two, to live before that vital organ gave out.

A heart transplant was a possibility, but Bella had such a rare blood type that it was unlikely a donor heart could be found before her heart failed.

She wanted to make peace with Bull before she died, but that was an iffy proposition at best. Besides, she was certain that once he knew the truth, he would insist that she conserve her strength. And she had four more children to get settled with loving spouses before she could rest.

Her machinations to get her youngest son Max together with his childhood sweetheart, Kristin Lassiter, had worked out perfectly. The two had recently married and were living happily ever after in Miami—along with the child that had come as a total surprise to her son, their precocious nine-year-old daughter Flick.

Bella had been using the services of Warren & Warren Investigations over the past several years to keep track of her wayward children, and the firm had done excellent work. She was certain Sam Warren would be able to locate the Ghost—if, indeed, it could be found.

The most recent report from the Texas-based private investigator had informed her that her second son, Riley, had left Hong Kong and joined her third son, Payne, on a boat off the coast of Turkey. Both sons were investigating ancient underwater ruins Riley had discovered while he'd been scuba diving. Hence her visit to Greece.

Riley was scheduled to return to his shipping base of operations on the island of Santorini in a month, and she was searching valiantly to discover what woman might have caught his eye over the past several years. Unfortunately, Riley's nearly constant travel kept him from meeting many eligible females. Her second son had always been a difficult child, inquisitive and intractable, and it was going to take a very special woman to capture his heart. Nevertheless, by the time Riley showed up here again, she hoped to have a match ready and waiting for him.

"Are you all right, Your Grace?" Emily asked.

Bella turned to find the assistant she'd hired when her heart had begun to fail standing at her shoulder.

Emily was a model of efficiency, considerate, always pleasant, and strangely devoted to Bella. She was thirty-two and unmarried, but Bella felt sure that if some man would just take the time to see past Emily's very plain face, he would find himself with a rare jewel.

"Is there anything I can do to help?" Emily asked.

"It seems Lydia borrowed the Ghost without asking, and it's been stolen from her. The thief contacted Bull asking for a ransom of twenty-five million dollars."

Emily gasped and the color drained from her face.

"I don't want Lydia to know that I know the truth," Bella continued. "I want her to come to me when the necklace has been recovered and tell me what she's done."

"When it's recovered, Your Grace?"

"Yes. I want you to contact Warren and Warren Investigations. I'm sure Sam Warren can—"

"I've already contacted him," Emily blurted. "I'm sorry, Your Grace, but Lydia called me when the necklace went missing. She begged me not to tell. She hoped to find it before you discovered it was missing. But now . . ."

"Now that's out of the question." Bella frowned and added, "Unless . . ."

"Unless what?"

"I presume that Sam Warren made a beeline for Rome."

"I told him that's where Lydia lost the necklace," Emily admitted.

"And he will contact you when the necklace has been found?"

"Yes, Your Grace."

"Then all we have to do is wait and let him do his job."

CHAPTER 11

"*W*hat made you want to be a private investigator?" Lydia asked Joe as their taxi rattled over Rome's black cobblestone streets toward the Westin Excelsior.

Joe shot her a sideways look. "I grew up with a father who investigated for a living."

"Of course! It's Warren *and* Warren investigations. How long have you and your dad worked together?"

"The name comes from my dad and my grandfather."

"Oh." Lydia waited for some elaboration on that statement, but Joe Warren was staring out the window at the many ancient facades bearing Corinthian or Ionian columns and the half-nude marble statues that made Rome such a fascinating city.

"Do you like this kind of work?" Lydia asked.

Joe shrugged. "I can take it or leave it."

"So why haven't you left it? I mean, if you really don't care for the job."

He put a hand on his injured leg and grimaced. "I don't have much choice. This leg won't allow me to do much else."

"How did you injure it?"

"IED," he said tersely.

Improvised Explosive Device. So he'd been a soldier. That explained the military camouflage he'd shown up wearing. "Is there any chance your mobility will improve?" she asked, eyeing his wounded limb.

"None," he said in a voice curt enough to shut off that line of questioning.

After growing up with four older brothers, Lydia wasn't cowed. She looked him in the eye and said, "You'd get around a lot better if you weren't too proud to use a cane."

He scowled but didn't contradict her.

"I'm an investigator myself," she said.

Joe raised a brow. "Then why do you need me?"

Lydia felt the flush rising on her cheeks and wasn't sure whether it was caused by Joe's intense, blue-eyed gaze or the fact that she'd given herself credit for being something she was not.

"What I mean is, I'm learning to be an investigator," she amended. "I'm following in the footsteps of my eldest brother Oliver. He can . . ." Her brother did his investigating on the sly and probably wouldn't appreciate her giving away his secret.

She glanced at Joe sideways and said, "The short answer to your question is that I need you because I'm not very good at this—yet. Lately I've been searching for a Toulouse Lautrec painting that was stolen from a museum in Paris, but without much success. Oliver would already have located—" Lydia cut herself off again. "Anyway, I'm learning as fast as I can."

"Why bother?"

"What do you mean?"

"You're beautiful. You're rich. You don't need to work."

Lydia heard the disdain in his voice and felt a surge of anger. "No, I don't need to work. I want to work. I want my life to have some meaning."

"There must be plenty of charities that would appreciate your efforts on their behalf."

"My brothers and I have formed a foundation that supports charitable work," she replied. "But finding a missing art treasure—something priceless and irreplaceable—and returning it, so the public can enjoy it again, is also worthwhile."

"Most museums have pretty good security," Joe said.

"You'd be surprised how ingenious thieves can be."

"Obviously," Joe said sardonically. "Since one managed to steal a priceless pearl right off your neck."

"I was drugged!" Lydia protested.

"You might want to consider the fact that whoever took the necklace knew where you were staying, because he made sure you got back to your hotel room. Very likely it was someone you know personally, since he didn't assault you when he had the chance."

Lydia stared at Joe wide-eyed. "You think a *friend* stole

the Ghost?"

Joe nodded. "Someone close to you, someone you'd never suspect. For reasons of privacy your hotel doesn't record who comes and goes, and no one at the front desk noticed you coming in last night, so you were apparently walking on your own two feet, most likely with someone else's help."

"How do you know all this? You slept the day away."

"I have an assistant in my office," Joe answered. "I called and got an update from her while you were talking with your fiancé."

"Harold isn't my fiancé," she objected.

"Fine. The guy who wants to marry you."

Lydia wasn't sure why it was so important to make it clear to Joe Warren that she wasn't attached, but she said, "Just because Harold wants to marry me doesn't mean I have any intention of marrying him."

"I see. Why settle for one man when you can have an army of them at your feet?"

"I'm not a flirt," Lydia said sharply. "And I don't sleep around."

"I never said you did."

But Lydia could see he was thinking it. She hated being put in a pigeonhole. "Harold doesn't want a wife. He wants a showpiece on his arm. How would you like it if a woman only wanted you for the financial security you could provide?"

Joe snorted. "Been there. Done that."

"And?"

"She walked away when it looked like I'd never walk again."

Lydia stared at him wide-eyed. "Someone rejected you?"

"Like day-old bread."

"I'm sorry."

"I'm not. Better to know up front that she wasn't the kind to stick for the long haul. Can we just drop it?"

So. He'd had his heart broken. And was still hurting, if she was any judge of the matter. "I'll never bring up the subject again," she said, "so long as you agree not to tar me with the same brush as the woman who walked away from you. I'm not like that."

Joe scoffed. "I haven't met the woman yet who—"

"Then I'm the first," she interrupted.

The taxi had stopped under the portico in front of the Westin Excelsior, and Joe got out. Lydia waited briefly to see if he was going to pay the driver or get her door, then realized she was on her own. She pulled a few euros from her purse to cover the fare and got out.

She was muttering to herself about Joe's manners when she realized he'd stopped to answer his phone, which had kept him from performing either service.

"Who is it?" she asked.

He held the phone against his chest as he crossed behind the taxi to join her. "My office." Then he put the phone to his ear again, said, "Uh-huh. Yeah. Roger that," and ended the call.

"What is it?" she asked anxiously. "Is there news about the Ghost?"

"Your dad got a call asking for a twenty-five million dollar ransom for the return of the Ghost. Your mother just hired my father's firm to find it."

Lydia's stomach twisted. "Oh, no! Daddy called me, and I lied about having the Ghost. Why didn't he confront me?" Then it dawned on her what Joe had just said. "My *father* got the ransom call, but my *mother* called to hire you? That must mean Daddy spoke with Mother. That's . . . amazing."

As far as Lydia knew her parents hadn't communicated directly in years. Maybe her loss of the Ghost was going to have at least one good result.

Joe put a hand to her back to usher her inside. His fingertips were resting in the hollow just above her buttocks, and Lydia felt a frisson of awareness skitter down her spine. She took an extra step to separate them as he said, "You find it *amazing* that your mother is speaking to your father?"

"Since my mother's assistant recommended you, I thought you must have worked for the Duchess in the past. In which case, you would know that my parents, who've been living apart for the past ten years, are famous—or rather, infamous—for avoiding each other while showing up at the same event with someone else."

Joe's eyes narrowed. "They must want to hurt each other pretty badly."

A shadow crossed Lydia's face. "Yes, they do."

Lydia realized Joe was headed directly for the front desk. "What are you doing?" she whispered. By the time she'd finished her sentence he was already speaking to the concierge.

Joe extended his hand, in which Lydia spied a folded fifty euro note, and said, "I believe you have a key for Sam Warren."

"Yes, sir. Here it is."

The concierge handed him a plastic card without giving the room number, and Joe put his hand to the small of Lydia's back again to head her toward the elevators. This time his little finger was definitely resting below her waist. She shot a look at him, wondering if he was touching her so intimately on purpose, but he seemed oblivious. Nevertheless, she took a step sideways to break the connection, which had her heart beating faster than she liked.

"That exchange at the front desk was odd," she said.

He cocked a brow. "In what way?"

"It felt very clandestine, like spy kind of stuff. I mean, announcing who you are and paying to receive a key card, especially if the room belongs to someone else."

"My assistant set the whole thing up. She's very thorough," Joe said as they entered the elevator. "The room is taken, but it's currently unoccupied."

As Lydia watched, Joe punched the button for the fifth floor. "I presume you know which lock fits that key?" she said.

"I do."

As they exited the elevator, Joe put his hand so low on her

back that Lydia realized he could likely feel the dimples above her buttocks. She turned to confront him and said, "I'll thank you to keep your hands to yourself!"

He looked affronted. "I have no idea what you're talking about."

"I'm talking about the way you put your hand on my—" Lydia wasn't sure what word to use. Derrière? Bottom? Butt?

He lifted both brows and stared back at her as though she were crazy. "I was trying to be a gentleman."

By putting your hand on my rear end? Lydia realized she was fighting a losing battle. "Never mind."

They'd stopped in front of a hotel room, and Joe slid the card into the slot. When the green light appeared, he held the door open for her and then followed her inside.

Lydia felt a chill of alarm because the unoccupied room bore clear signs of its occupant, which brought home the fact that they'd broken into someone's room.

She spied an open Coke can and a half-filled glass of Coke on the end table next to the unmade canopied bed, along with an open paperback mystery by a famous British author. She peered into the bathroom and saw a bottle of Gucci male cologne, shaving cream, a razor, and a toothbrush. An open computer sat on the desk together with yesterday's London *Times*. Did that make the room's occupant British? Was it possible Joe was right, and the thief was someone she knew? Someone she'd grown up with in England?

She turned and asked, "What are we doing here?"

"My assistant traced an email offering the Ghost for sale to the business center at this hotel." Joe headed straight to the desk, sat in the chair, turned on the computer, and began clicking the mouse. "She checked the hotel's guest registration—"

"Is that legal? To hack into the hotel's records?"

"Do you want the Ghost back?"

It took her a moment to work out what he hadn't said. "Who's staying in this room?"

"Your British cousin."

Lydia took a few steps backward and sank onto the bed. While she had numerous American relations on her father's side, she had only one cousin on her mother's side. "Gabe?"

"Gabriel Alexander Wharton, to be precise," Joe replied. "Your aunt Alicia's bastard son."

"That's an awful way to refer to Gabe."

"Bastard. Illegitimate. Tomato. Tomahto."

Lydia pursed her lips. Aunt Alicia was her mother's twin sister, and the truth was, she hadn't been married when Gabe was born. Lydia wasn't sure why, but the two sisters had been estranged for as long as she could remember. She'd once tried to broach the issue with her mother, but the Duchess's eyes had looked so agonized, she'd quickly dropped the subject.

Alicia had been born five minutes after Bella, but because she'd come second, Bella had inherited the title of duchess and the Blackthorne estate, while Alicia had been left with only what Bella saw fit to give her. In the beginning, because the estate had been in decline, there had been nothing to share. Bull's infusion of cash had allowed Blackthorne Abbey, the ancestral home of the Dukes of Blackthorne, to be opulently refurbished, but Aunt Alicia had left the Abbey shortly after Bull and Bella's marriage and never returned.

Lydia caught herself chewing on her thumbnail and yanked it out of her mouth.

"Is this him?" Joe said, holding up his phone so Lydia could see the picture that had apparently been sent to Joe by his assistant.

"Yes." Lydia hadn't seen Gabriel since he was a teenager, and she gasped at the amazing resemblance between her cousin Gabe and her brother Oliver, except that Gabe had blue eyes while Oliver had brown. Their similar features might have been due to the fact that they had twin sisters for mothers. But the two men might have been twins themselves, they looked so much alike. Which suggested they might have more than a mother in common. Lydia felt dizzy at the unwilling conclusion her mind had drawn: *Oliver and Gabe had the same father.*

Lydia shivered. Oliver and Gabe were the same age, and it was horrible to think that the same scoundrel—he hadn't married either twin—might have impregnated both her mother and her aunt within the period of a year. Now *that* was a mystery it would be interesting to solve. Except that Oliver, who was an amazing investigator, seemed never to have investigated his own birth. Better not to stick her nose into his business.

"Take a look around," Joe said as he settled in at Gabe's computer.

"What is it I'm supposed to find?" she asked as she rose and began rummaging through drawers.

"Anything that tells us where Gabe might be keeping the Ghost or information about anyone he might have communicated with in order to sell it on the black market."

Lydia took inventory of where things were when she opened a drawer to be sure she could put items back the same way after she'd gone through them. "I thought you said the thief asked Daddy for a ransom."

"He may very well intend to collect from your father as well as a buyer who wants the necklace."

Lydia hissed in a breath. It was bad enough that her father might have to pay to get the Ghost back. But it was only money, and Bull Benedict had plenty of it. The thought that the Ghost might never be recovered made her blood run cold. "I can't believe my own cousin would have drugged me and stolen the Ghost."

"Did you see him at the charity ball? Did you speak to him?"

"Everyone was wearing masks."

"You didn't recognize his voice?"

Lydia paused to think. She tried to remember if anyone she'd met that evening—especially anyone who'd offered her a drink—reminded her of her cousin but came up blank. "I had no inkling he was there. But I haven't seen him since we were kids. He went to private school—that's what we call a public school in England—and I went to a boarding school in Switzerland."

"Of course you did."

Lydia ignored the sarcasm in Joe's voice and continued, "As far as I know, neither Gabe nor his mother has been in touch with my family for years. I mean, how could he know I'd be wearing the Ghost? I wasn't even sure I could get it from the vault in England."

"Sounds like a crime of opportunity," Joe mused.

"What do you mean?"

"He saw the necklace and acted on the spur of the moment."

"Are you suggesting he was carrying rohypnol, or something like it, around with him?"

Joe nodded. "He was probably planning to rob—or rape—someone. He just happened to choose you. Would he have recognized the necklace?"

Lydia made a face. "Probably. Maybe. My mother's worn it to several high-profile events."

Lydia was having trouble imagining her cousin being the kind of person who would drug a woman to steal from her—or worse. She couldn't believe he would purposely drug his own cousin to steal a priceless piece of jewelry. But the fact that she'd gotten back to her hotel safely and hadn't been ravished suggested a thief with some consideration for her.

Which made her wonder if her cousin might be the culprit.

She frowned at an expensive printed invitation she found in the drawer of the bedside table. She had an invitation to the same charity event.

At that moment, the phone rang. Lydia turned to stare at it, then turned to Joe. "Should we answer that? Is it some kind of signal from the concierge that Gabe is back?"

Joe swore under his breath as he shut down Gabe's computer and rose. "I didn't make any arrangements with the concierge, but I don't think we should take any chances. Let's go."

Before either of them could move, Lydia heard the key card being inserted in the lock.

CHAPTER 12

*J*oe turned off the computer and jumped up in the same instant. He grabbed Lydia by the hand as she slammed a drawer closed and hauled her toward the French doors that led to the balcony. He opened the unlocked door and shoved her out ahead of him, then eased the door closed and hustled her toward one of the tall, potted cyprus bushes that flanked the French doors.

His damned leg gave out, and he ended up body-to-body with her against the stone wall. He pressed himself closer to be sure they were hidden behind the narrow bush, ignoring her indignant look. When she opened her mouth in what he suspected was a protest, he shut her up by kissing her.

He thrust his tongue into her mouth, and she tasted as sweet as he'd imagined. He felt the softness of her breasts crushed against his chest and fit his hard body into the cradle of her thighs. He hadn't been able to stop himself from reaching out to touch her all day, and he smiled inwardly as he remembered how she'd called him on it. One moment she was kissing him back, and in the next, Joe felt as though he were tangling with a wildcat.

Lydia bit his lip, and he tasted blood. One of her hands grasped his hair while the nails of the other dug deep into his shoulder. She bucked against him, and Joe felt his body throb. His hand closed over her breast, and his thumb brushed a nipple that budded responsively beneath his touch.

He froze when he heard the French doors click open and struggled to control his breathing. He broke the kiss and laid a fingertip against Lydia's lips to caution her to silence. Her eyes went wide as she turned her head toward the door. Joe held his breath waiting to see whether they would be discovered. To his relief, Gabriel Wharton never came into view. Apparently he'd headed toward the other side of the balcony.

"I've had a few bites from potential buyers," he heard Gabe say, "but I think Bull is going to provide the real payoff."

Lydia whimpered, and he put a hand over her mouth to silence her. She tried to yank his hand away, but when he shook his head, she stilled.

"No, Mother, I don't think it would be better to sell the Ghost to someone else," Gabe said. "Bull owes me and you both after what he did to you." He made an angry sound in his throat. "The man is my father, too! I should get some of what he's given to his other children."

Joe felt Lydia stiffen at this announcement. She struggled

briefly before he used the weight of his body to press her more tightly against the wall. He narrowed his eyes in warning, and she froze, but her eyes spoke livid volumes. Clearly, she hadn't been aware that her father had sired a bastard son with her mother's twin. And she wasn't happy about it.

"I promise you the Ghost is safely hidden." Gabe made an exasperated sound, then added, "I'm not a complete idiot, Mother. Can't you just, for once in your life, trust me?" He hesitated, apparently listening, then replied, "It's better if you don't know. Stop worrying. Nothing's going to happen to me. I'll see you tonight at the gala."

Joe heard footsteps on the flagstone before Gabe reentered his room and closed the balcony door behind him. Joe waited to see whether he would lock the door, but it remained unsecured, as it had been when they'd left the room. Joe couldn't imagine anyone leaving the balcony doors unlocked if a necklace worth a fortune was secreted in the room. Ergo, the Ghost was hidden somewhere else.

When he focused his gaze back on Lydia, Joe realized that whatever magic had caused her to respond to his kiss had passed. Her body was rigid, and her palms were pressed flat against his chest. His lips curved cynically. She was as cold now as she'd been hot before. He supposed she'd realized just who she'd been kissing. Not some lord, but a lowly Delta sergeant.

"How long am I going to be stuck here with you?" she hissed when he took his hand from her mouth.

"Not a second longer than necessary," he shot back.

Joe kept their bodies close as he pulled out his cell phone and called his sister. "I need you to have the front desk call Gabe Wharton and get him out of his room."

"I warned you to be quick," Sam replied.

"Look, I'm trapped on the balcony with Lydia. Can you help me, or not?"

Joe stared at Lydia, who glared back at him. Her arms remained wedged between them while they waited for the phone to ring in Gabriel's room.

Lydia had managed to separate their upper bodies, but his hips remained tight against hers. She'd wriggled once but gasped and stopped moving when she realized his body was still hard as a rock. She never lowered her gaze, just kept her amazing violet eyes trained on his, daring him to do his worst.

Joe admired her gumption, but he wasn't about to give her the satisfaction of telling her so.

"My father never had relations with my aunt," Lydia said quietly but emphatically. "He loves my mother too much to ever do that to her."

"Whatever you say," Joe replied in an equally soft voice. "But your cousin seemed pretty sure of himself."

"Gabe looks exactly like my eldest brother," she said. "And Oliver *isn't* my father's son."

Joe lifted a brow at that interesting tidbit of information. He wished his sister were here instead of him. Sam knew all the ins and outs of this family. He was pretty much constantly out on a limb. He didn't want to step amiss, so he said, "You're sure about that?"

"Oliver's eyes are dark brown," she said. When he just stared at her she added, "Both of my parents have blue eyes."

Joe nodded as he did the genetic math. But he couldn't resist pointing out, "Gabe has blue eyes."

Lydia looked anxious as she said, "It can't be true. I don't believe it. My father was deeply in love with my mother when Oliver was born—and Gabe is the same age."

"If you say so."

She pressed her lips flat and stared at him through narrowed eyes without saying another word.

It wasn't more than another minute before the phone trilled, but it seemed much longer, because he never stopped wanting to put himself inside her, never stopped wanting to see the ecstasy on her face when she climaxed.

He waited another minute, then checked to make sure Gabe was gone before he and Lydia entered, and then exited, the room. They took the stairs down so they wouldn't run into her cousin on the elevator.

Before they entered the lobby, Joe checked to make sure Gabe wasn't around, and they left and caught a cab out front, heading back to Lydia's hotel.

"Did you get anything useful from Gabe's computer?" Lydia asked.

It seemed she was going to avoid mentioning the whole

kissing incident, which was fine with him. "I set it up so my sis—" Joe caught himself and finished, "So my assistant can remotely view his computer. If he sends or receives any correspondence regarding the sale of the Ghost, we'll know about it. How about you? Did you find anything?"

"I found an invitation to a charity event being held tonight. It might be the gala where Gabe plans to meet his mother."

"That sounds promising. Can we just show up? Or do we need an invitation to get in?"

"I've already got an invitation."

"How fancy is this thing?"

Lydia shot him an amused look. "You're going to have to wear a tux."

CHAPTER 13

*L*ydia claimed the bathroom first. She debated whether to lock the door, since Joe was dressing in her room as well, but in the end, decided against it. "He wouldn't dare," she muttered as she clipped her hair up off her neck. She stripped herself bare, then stepped into the steaming shower. A moment later she heard the bathroom door open and peeked around the shower curtain to find Joe standing at the sink wearing nothing but a towel slung low on his hips.

She angled the white cloth curtain to cover her naked body, stuck her head out, and stated the obvious. "I'm in here."

"It'll save time if I shave while you shower," he said as he picked up the electric razor she'd provided, plugged it in, and turned it on.

Lydia stared in disbelief for a moment, then said, "I prefer to shower *alone.*"

"You *are* in the shower alone," he pointed out. "I'm standing out here in front of the sink. But I'd be happy to join you."

When Joe turned off the razor and took a step toward her, Lydia dropped the shower curtain back into place with a throaty *grr-r-r* of frustration. She grabbed a washcloth and the small, fragrant bar of soap and began viciously soaping the wet cloth. She thought she heard Joe chuckle before the annoying buzz of the electric razor began again.

Lydia realized she was going to have to wait for Joe to finish shaving and leave the bathroom before she could get out, so she took her time, soaping every inch of herself from top to bottom. She was still covered with suds when the buzz abruptly stopped.

"If you're done, you can leave," she called out to him.

A moment later, the shower curtain was shoved back and Joe—naked as a jaybird—joined her.

Lydia grabbed the curtain and covered herself, flustered and furious. "Get out! Go!"

"I'm already wet. Might as well get clean."

She gaped at him, which was when she realized that, for the first time since she'd met him, she could see the contours of his face. He'd left only a day's worth of stubble, just enough to shadow his jaw and make him look uncivilized. Dangerous. Like the rogue he was.

Her eyes slid down to his broad, muscular chest, which possessed a V of dark curls, and followed the trail of the jagged scar that ran at an angle from his collarbone, across a six-pack of abs, all the way to his navel. Lydia resisted the strong urge to touch.

Joe eased the washcloth from her hand, snatched the soap from the ceramic dish, sniffed it, scrunched up his nose at the smell, then began making a lather. "Faster if we do this together."

Lydia recovered her senses and snarled, "I can't believe you have the gall to—"

"By the way," he said with a grin. "I can see your fanny. Very nice."

Lydia yelped and grabbed more of the curtain in an attempt to conceal her backside. She heard Joe gasp and realized she'd inadvertently exposed a pink nipple.

Joe's response was instantly—and impressively—visible.

Lydia felt a curl of desire begin in her womb as her body reacted viscerally to the sight of his arousal. Her heartbeat shot up as though she'd been running a mile, and she was having trouble catching her breath. When she was able to focus her gaze back on Joe's face, she saw his eyes were heavy-lidded, his pupils huge black pools in a sea of blue as they drank in the sight of her.

Lydia let go of the curtain.

Joe reached for her without speaking.

She'd expected him to rush, but he took his time, drawing lazy circles around her slick breasts. His eyes followed the direction of his callused hand as his palm slid down the center of her taut body, creating responsive quivers, until he reached his destination.

Lydia moaned, and Joe captured the sound with his mouth, as he worked wonderful magic with his fingers.

Lydia was shocked at how wet she was and how quickly she climaxed. Joe made a satisfied sound in his throat as he released her. Lydia's knees threatened to collapse, but strong arms rescued her. Joe drew her close, so she could feel the hot, hard length of him against her hip.

Lydia hands circled Joe's neck, and she grasped the hair at his nape, which was both still dry and surprisingly soft. She held on tight as their tongues dueled. She gave as good as she got, fighting to stay in control, refusing to surrender, uncertain why it mattered but knowing she couldn't give in.

Joe made a guttural sound as he tore his mouth from hers. His lazy-lidded gaze locked on her face as his nostrils flared for the scent of her. He suddenly picked her up, elbowed the lever off and the curtain aside, then stepped out of the shower. She could feel the heat coming off of his body, feel the muscle and sinew in the arms that held her close. She'd forgotten completely about Joe's injured leg until he swore under his breath and faltered halfway across the bedroom, almost dropping her.

She struggled to be set down, worried that he would fall. "I can walk."

His grip tightened as he said, "I've got you."

Luckily, they were only a few steps from the bed, and he settled onto the edge of it with her in his lap. She'd grasped him around the neck when he'd almost fallen, so she felt the terrible tension in his shoulders.

She put a hand to his cheek and forced him to look at her.

"It's all right. So you have a bum leg. It's no big deal."

"Maybe not to you," he shot back. "It's altered my life so completely I don't recognize myself anymore."

He turned his face away, and she realized he hadn't meant to reveal quite so much of the agony beneath the composed surface he presented to the world.

"A lot of guys have come home in a lot worse shape than I'm in," he admitted in a low, harsh voice. "I guess I should be thankful I can walk at all."

She hesitated, then said, "But you can't help regretting what's been lost."

She heard him swallow hard and realized he was fighting to subdue his emotions. He glanced at her but said nothing, which revealed the depth of the struggle within him.

Lydia was moved by the fact that a man as physically strong as Joe had admitted to any sort of vulnerability. It made him more human, more sympathetic. It made her want to offer comfort. It made her want to share her own vulnerability.

But it felt too dangerous—she was far too frightened— to admit to her own foibles. She'd never let anyone, not her family, not her friends, and especially not any man she'd dated, see her insecurities. The men she'd allowed into her life had no inkling of the unloved and unlovable girl hiding behind a façade of extraordinary beauty and icy sophistication.

The moment when she might have shared her fears with Joe came and went. She yearned for the closeness she'd let slip away and settled for pressing a tender kiss on his throat beneath his ear. He stiffened for an instant, and she could tell he was debating whether to stop what he'd started in the shower. She could feel his erection throb beneath her thigh and pressed more soft kisses across his throat and chin and cheeks, until she finally reached his mouth.

He was hungry for her, his thrusting tongue seeking the honey to be found within.

Lydia gave in to the desire to be joined with this man, who'd let her see behind the shield of strength and power that most men of her acquaintance wore. She turned to straddle Joe, leading him inside where she wanted him, moaning as their bodies became joined, so they were one.

Their loving was gentle and tender. And savage and satisfying. Joe took her to places she had never been. Teased and touched and taunted, giving her pleasure—and joy—almost beyond endurance. Until at last she lay in his embrace, lungs heaving, completely sated.

Lydia had made love before, but she couldn't remember wanting to give so much of herself to another human being. Or allowing herself to feel quite so much. What did it mean?

Lydia was afraid to look at Joe, afraid to discover that he'd retreated behind the stone wall that had come down during their lovemaking. She waited with bated breath to see what he would do next.

"We're going to be late," he said, his fingers gently brushing a few sweaty strands of hair from her brow and setting a kiss in its place.

It felt like love, even though she knew that was impossible, considering the circumstances. "I don't care if we're late," she murmured, too languorous to move. She pressed her nose against his throat, treasuring the closeness she felt towards him. It amazed her to think that Joe Warren, with whom she'd shared her body—and who was threatening to steal her soul—had been a stranger a mere twenty-four hours ago. She felt as though she'd fallen under some sort of spell. How else could she explain capitulating to such a ruffian?

She felt a deep sadness, because she knew that the love-making—and the feeling of being loved—that she'd just experienced, shattering though it had been, wasn't likely to be repeated. She and Joe would find the Ghost in the next forty-eight hours, or they would not. Whatever the case, in two days he would walk out of her life, and she would never see him again. There was no sense fantasizing about some sort of happily ever after. It wasn't going to happen.

The certain knowledge that Joe would be gone soon gave her the courage to say, "I've never met anyone like you."

He made a disgruntled sound in his throat.

"I mean that in a good way," she quickly added. She leaned up on an elbow so she could look into his eyes which, despite their ice-blue color, seemed filled with warmth. "I have a hard time trusting men, which is why I never do things like this."

"*This* being *sex?*" Joe clarified.

"Sex with someone I just met," Lydia said to make her meaning clear. It wasn't that he hadn't given her a choice. He simply hadn't been shy about reaching for what he wanted. "You're not what I thought you were."

"What was that?"

"A hoodlum," she said with a smile to ease the sting of the insult. "You don't follow the rules."

"What rules?" he said.

"Of civilized society."

"I can't pretend to be what I'm not. If I'm not good enough for you—"

She put her fingertips across his lips. "Class has nothing to do with it."

He arched a disbelieving brow.

"It's the way you make me feel. Like . . ."

He kissed her fingertips, then threaded their fingers together as he asked, "Like what?"

Lydia became aware of a sudden knot in her throat. She was terrified of telling him too much. Terrified of revealing how much she wanted to be loved and how much she feared she never would be. She swallowed painfully and said, "I feel like you're seeing *me*, and not Lady Lydia, the Duchess of Blackthorne's wayward daughter."

"What's the difference?" he asked.

Lydia smiled. "It speaks volumes that you don't have a clue."

He gently brushed her hair away from her face and asked, "What time does this charity shindig start?"

"Seven o'clock."

"We'd better get a move on," he said as he untangled their hands. He rose, completely unashamed of his nakedness.

For the first time, Lydia saw the full extent of the damage to his leg. It was a wonder he could walk at all. She opened her mouth to remark on it but decided he was well aware of the problem. Instead she asked, "What time is it?"

He looked at his battered watch. "Five past six."

"Oh, my God. How did it get so late?" Lydia bolted upright, realized she was naked, and grabbed at the sheet.

Joe grinned and said, "You're more of a distraction than I counted on."

Lydia winced at the dismissal of what they'd just done as a "distraction." She wondered if the hurt she felt had shown on her face because he suddenly leaned over and kissed her softly on the mouth.

"Come on, baby," he said in a husky voice. "Time for work."

Lydia felt the ache in her heart ease. She hadn't been called "baby" since she was one. It felt strange . . . and strangely nice.

She let go of the sheet and stepped out of bed. What was the expression her father used? No sense closing the barn door after the cows are gone. She smiled when she saw Joe's body respond to the sight of her. She turned her back on him, feeling a prickly awareness of his gaze on her as she headed into the bathroom.

This time she shut the door. And locked it.

$\mathcal{L}$ydia did a slow inspection of Joe Warren as they waited their turn to be admitted to the ballroom at another of Rome's five-star hotels, where the charity gala was being held. She had to admit she was impressed. Joe had frowned ferociously when she suggested that a tailor should come to the hotel to make sure his tux fit impeccably.

"Think of it as camouflage you need to invade enemy territory," she'd said with a smile meant to encourage his cooperation. "Even though your tux is rented, it can't look like it's rented."

Joe had nodded curtly, and she'd called her father's tailor in Rome before the PI could change his mind. The effort had been worth it. The tux emphasized Joe's sculpted shoulders, his narrow waist, and his long legs—all of which she could mentally see beneath the fitted cloth.

In the light from the chandelier she could see, beneath the

shadow of beard, the whitened scars that reminded her he'd been a warrior.

Lydia found herself remembering how that male bristle had felt against her naked flesh. Joe turned suddenly to look at her, and she flushed, afraid that he'd somehow read her mind.

She stared straight ahead, but she could feel his eyes on her, doing the same sort of slow assessment she'd done of him, from her low-cut bodice to the violet silk that sheathed her hips. It wasn't an entirely uncomfortable experience, because Lydia had discovered, to her dismay, that she *wanted* Joe Warren to like what he saw.

Which made no sense.

The man had been nothing but trouble from the moment she'd met him. Joe Warren would be in her life only until she achieved her goal of retrieving the Ghost. He lived in America, for heaven's sake! Other than family trips to her father's ancestral home in Richmond, Virginia, she'd spent as little time in the United States as possible. She'd been raised in Great Britain and Europe and had always imagined herself living there forever after.

There was no possibility of a life with Joe on her side of the pond, either. He would never fit in with her crowd. His military service had apparently made him efficient and effective. But his manners were rough, and he brooked no nonsense. Lydia's friends didn't quite lead frivolous lives, but many of them were wealthy enough to enjoy lifestyles oriented more towards fun than work.

Lydia felt Joe's eyes on her, and a frisson of excitement ran down her spine, as though his callused hands were actually touching her. Lydia didn't dare look at him, because she was sure he'd be able to tell the effect he had on her. She'd set boundaries all her life to keep men at arm's length, but nothing she did seemed to matter where Joe was concerned. He'd simply stepped past the barriers she'd established as though they didn't exist.

The most disturbing thing was that she'd liked his kisses and enjoyed his touch. No, that wasn't true. She'd *loved* his kisses and *reveled* in his touch. Lydia was so used to men being intimidated by her beauty, so used to men wanting her approval, that she wasn't quite sure how to handle a man who took what he wanted and brought her along for the joyous ride.

Lydia started when Joe took her hand in his, threading their fingers together again as he had in bed, reminding her of the intimacy they'd shared. He handed their invitation to the greeter at the door, then tugged to keep her beside him as they entered the glittering ballroom.

She turned to glare at him for pulling her along like a dog on a leash, but he forestalled her by muttering, "My leg's killing me."

Her eyes narrowed as she stared down at their joined hands and then at his wounded leg. That damaged leg seemed to provide excuses for all sorts of behavior. He'd managed fine all the way here. He'd managed fine standing in line. He took a halting step, and she pursed her lips, remember how he'd almost fallen carrying her from the shower to the bed.

Maybe he was telling the truth. But if he was in pain, it was his own fault. Before they'd left the hotel room, she'd offered him the cane she'd bought for him, and he'd refused it yet again.

Lydia purposefully ignored the man holding her hand, focusing on the activity in the ballroom. A small orchestra was performing a romantic tune, and several couples occupied the dance floor. She couldn't help wondering whether Joe could dance, and whether he would take her in his arms before the night was out.

Under her breath she said, "Bad idea, Lydia." She needed to keep as much space between herself and Joe Warren as she could manage until the job was done and he was gone.

"What did you say?"

"Nothing." She turned her head away from Joe, eyeing the silent auction set up on tables along the outside of the room. Round tables for ten with elaborate centerpieces were arranged in the center of the ballroom for the dinner to come. Lydia hadn't planned to attend this event, so they would likely end up seated with strangers, which was fine, as far as she was concerned. She didn't want anyone she knew seeing her with Joe. The fewer explanations she had to make, the better.

"Lydia!"

Lydia turned toward the shocked voice and was surprised to find her would-be fiancé standing not ten feet away. She tried to free her hand from Joe's, but his grip tightened. She gave up, smiled brightly at Harold, and said, "I didn't expect to see you here."

Harold stared pointedly at their joined hands. "Obviously. What is it with you and this . . . gentleman?" Harold spat the word as though Joe was anything but.

"The lady's made her feelings plain," Joe said. "She doesn't want anything to do with you. Beat it."

Lydia was shocked at Joe's abrupt dismissal of Harold, and it was clear from the way Harold's jaw clamped tight that he was furious at such unaccustomed treatment.

Harold's shoulders squared as he demanded, "Who the bloody hell do you think you are?"

Lydia gasped at the profanity. She could count on one hand the number of times she'd heard Harold swear—and two of those fingers could be attributed directly to Joe Warren.

"Nobody who would interest you," Joe replied without rancor. He turned to Lydia and said, "Would you like to dance?"

Lydia was struggling not to laugh at the look of incredulity on Harold's face. "Yes, I would."

Joe limped off toward the dance floor without a backward glance at Harold, dragging her along behind him. Lydia snuck a look back at Harold, who was glaring daggers at Joe's back.

When they reached the dance floor, Joe set a hand at her waist, then took their joined hands and leaned them against his shoulder. They began to move to the evocative song the orchestra was playing. Her head came only to Joe's chin, and she was very much aware of feeling protected in his embrace. She met his gaze and said, "That was brazen."

He arched a questioning brow.

"Harold is used to men deferring to him, not dismissing him out of hand."

"He was out of line," Joe said. "No means no."

Lydia smiled ruefully. "Except where you're concerned."

"I haven't heard that word come out of your mouth."

"I—" Lydia realized she'd never actually told him no. When she could have spoken on Gabe's balcony, he hadn't given her the chance, and she'd been too shocked in the shower. But there had been plenty of opportunities later to put him off, and she hadn't. "You're nothing like the men I know."

"You're not exactly what I would choose, either."

Lydia's face flushed at the rebuff. She hadn't meant her statement as a criticism, but his sounded very much like one.

"Then it's a good thing you won't need to spend any more time with me once you find the Ghost."

He responded to the anger in her voice by pulling her close, so she could feel his hardened shaft against her belly. He growled in her ear, "That's what you do to me. Every time I think of you. Every time I look at you. Do you blame me if I don't like it? I'm not used to wanting a woman like that, and I'll be damned if I'll play games with a spoiled brat. I'd be happy to lay you down and put myself inside you again. All you have to do is say the word. But don't expect me to kowtow to you because you're a society girl and I'm a simple soldier." He made an unpleasant sound in his throat and amended, "*Was* a simple soldier."

Lydia felt breathless, and her heart was pounding in her chest. She was frightened by such plain speaking. And aroused by it. "I don't like the way you make me feel, either," she shot back.

He merely raised a brow, waiting for her to continue, waiting for her to admit that she wanted him, too. Lydia had met plenty of arrogant men in her life, but Joe's self-confidence seemed to come from something other than conceit. He was as far from someone she would have chosen for herself as daylight was from dark. And she was no more willing to kowtow to him than he was to her.

Maybe you've met your match.

The thought came unwillingly. Lydia shivered at the thought that private investigator Joe Warren should be the man who threatened her carefully guarded heart.

With her parents as an example, Lydia didn't believe in a love that lasted forever. Passion was possible and laudable and could exist for brief episodes. But loving a man could only result in eventual heartbreak. Which was why Lydia had made it a point never to get involved emotionally.

So how had Joe Warren managed so quickly—in a single day—to get under her skin and threaten her heart? The thought of the disaster that lay in wait made her shudder. She needed to find the Ghost and get Joe Warren out of her life.

Lydia realized her body was still pressed against Joe's and

stiffened in his arms.

He released her and took a step back. "I take it you're done dancing."

She nodded curtly.

"Guess we'd better find a place to sit."

To Lydia's dismay, he took her hand in his again, and she couldn't help enjoying the warmth and the strength of his grasp. She stayed close to Joe, smiling at a couple she recognized without introducing her escort. She didn't realize where they were headed until they ended up at a table where her aunt Alicia sat next to her cousin Gabe.

"Lydia! What a nice surprise!" her aunt said. "I hope you can join us." She gestured to the two empty seats that remained next to her at the table, which was otherwise full.

"We'd love to," Lydia said as she glanced at Joe. What on earth was Joe thinking, bringing them to this table? How was she going to introduce him without giving away his purpose for being here? She avoided looking at Gabe as Joe pulled out her chair so she could sit down next to her aunt.

"Who is this with you?" her aunt asked, right on cue.

Lydia had opened her mouth to reply when Joe said, "Lydia and I are working on a project together."

Lydia knew what question was coming next.

When Gabe asked, "Really? What sort of project?" she lifted a brow and waited to see how Joe, who was seating himself, would answer.

Joe smiled, revealing very white, very straight teeth,

and said, "We're investigating the theft of a painting from a museum in Paris." He looked directly at Gabe and added, "Purely for fun, of course."

Lydia had registered the audible gasp from Gabe when Joe said "theft" and the quieter exhale that followed when he said "painting." Gabe's shoulders tensed when Joe added, "Purely for fun," as though Joe had actually said, "And we're coming after *you*."

Lydia realized why Gabe had felt so threatened when she turned to look at Joe. There was nothing relaxed about Joe's posture. He looked like a lion ready to pounce.

"How is your mother?" Aunt Alicia asked. "More to the point, *where* is your mother? I haven't seen her for ages."

Lydia was disconcerted by both questions. She wasn't sure how to answer the first—and didn't have a clue about the second. "Mother is fine," she said. "She's been traveling quite a bit. She was at the Seasons for Mother's Day."

She knew that much because she'd been invited to join her mother and had found a reason—as had her four brothers, who'd also been invited—not to show up. Lydia had been appalled when she's realized during the Skyped meeting of the Castle Foundation that every one of them had abandoned the Duchess on Mother's Day. But the request had come so late, and been made in such an offhand way that, at the time, it hadn't seemed important to be there. Lydia suddenly wondered if there had been some significance to the invitation.

Unfortunately, she couldn't ask her mother anything

until she'd recovered the Ghost and returned it to the vault at Blackthorne Abbey.

She felt Joe's hand on her thigh and realized he expected her to take advantage of the opportunity he'd given her to question her aunt. She included both Gabe and her aunt in her gaze as she asked, "What brings you two to Rome?"

They both answered at the same time. And gave two different answers.

CHAPTER 15

*J*oe's leg was killing him, but it had been worth it to hold Lydia close as they danced. He hadn't meant to tell her how much he wanted—needed—to put himself inside her, but he wasn't sorry about that, either. If she had a stitch on under that form-fitting dress, he'd eat a rattlesnake raw. His mind's eye had provided an exquisite picture of her stark naked, and it took all his willpower to resist the urge to throw her over his shoulder and haul her off to one of the rooms upstairs.

He smiled wryly. That would be some trick. His bad leg had already proved it wasn't up to the task, and it was throbbing right now like it might explode. He stared at the champagne flute and the empty wine glass stationed next to his plate and realized he needed something stronger to assuage the pain, or he wasn't going to make it through the evening.

He was summoning a waiter when Lydia asked Gabe and his mother what they were doing in Rome, but his attention swerved back to the two thieves when they gave two different answers to her question.

"We're on holiday," Alicia said.

"We're looking at investment opportunities," Gabe said.

Joe had to give Alicia credit. She didn't even glance at Gabe as she produced a feline smile and said, "Well, *I'm* on holiday. My son is the one who insists on making it a working vacation." Then she looked Joe in the eye and added, "I didn't realize Lydia had a private investigator working for her."

"Not *for* her," Joe corrected. "*With* her."

Alicia gave Lydia a baleful look. "Where did you meet this fellow?"

Lydia wasn't nearly as good at lying as her aunt was. Her gaze shot away from Alicia for a second, a dead giveaway that whatever she said next was pure fiction. When Lydia finally made eye contact with her aunt, she said, "Joe is a friend of one of my American cousins."

Joe felt a jolt of alarm, because he had no idea who Lydia's American cousins were, although Alicia surely must. His sister had given him a rundown on all the supposed players in this little drama, but Lydia's American relations hadn't been mentioned.

"We ran into each other at that masquerade ball held earlier this week," Joe said. "It turned out we had Lydia's American cousin—and a desire to play private detective—in common."

"Didn't I see you there?" Lydia asked Gabe.

Gabe looked startled but said nothing.

"I was sure it was you," Lydia persisted with a smile meant to disarm him.

Gabe's eyes narrowed to slits. "How did you know it was me? We were all masked. And why didn't you say hello?"

Joe waited to see how Lydia was going to get herself out of the hole she'd dug. She'd already admitted to Joe that she couldn't have recognized her cousin's voice, and if Gabe pressed, she wouldn't be able to describe his mask or costume, either. More to the point, if she'd recognized him, why hadn't she acknowledged him?

She reached out and laid a hand on Gabe's arm, ramped up the wattage on her smile, and said, "You're taller than just about anyone I know, and you have the same habit as Oliver."

"What's that?" Gabe asked.

"I don't know how to describe it, exactly," she said. "It's the way you stand with your feet widespread and your shoulders back, as though you own the world." She laughed, a tinkling sound that send a shiver of sexual awareness racing down Joe's spine.

Joe saw Gabe stiffen, as though he knew exactly what Lydia meant, which suggested that she might actually have noted his presence at the event.

"I didn't say hello to you because I was busy flirting with Joe." Lydia removed her hand from Gabe's sleeve and twined her fingers with Joe's.

"Was that your mother's necklace I saw around your throat?" Gabe asked, conceding by his question that he'd not only been there but had noticed Lydia. "The Ghost, I think it's called."

Joe felt Lydia's fingernails dig into his palm as Gabe ventured further into the risky game they were playing.

"Why, yes, it was," Lydia replied.

Joe could see her pulse racing in her throat and wondered whether she was going to admit that the Ghost had been stolen.

Lydia stepped back from the brink, saying instead, "I plan to wear it to another event next week."

"Which event is that?" Alicia asked.

"The World Health Gala," Lydia said.

Alicia smiled, but there was nothing friendly in the expression. "I would love to see the Ghost again. It's been years since your mother wore it."

"You should come," Lydia said. "I'm sure I could get you an invitation."

"I'll let you know if I can fit it into my schedule." Alicia rose and said, "I think I'll take a look at the items up for bid at the silent auction." She focused her gaze on her son and added, "I believe there were a couple of items you were interested in, Gabe. Will you join me?"

"Of course, Mother," Gabe said, standing and offering his mother his arm.

Joe watched them until they were out of hearing and then said to Lydia, "What was it you hoped to gain by telling Gabe you saw him at the event where the Ghost was stolen?"

"I got him to admit he was there," Lydia said.

"To what purpose?"

Lydia withdrew her hand from his, and Joe immediately felt the loss. She raised her chin and said, "I want him to know that I know that he took it."

"That's just going to make him more careful."

"On the other hand, he might do something rash," Lydia countered. "Like lead us to wherever he's hiding the Ghost."

Joe had been talking to Lydia, but he'd been watching Alicia and Gabe. "You just might be right."

"What?"

"They're leaving the ballroom. Come on, let's go."

Joe slid his arm around Lydia's waist as they headed for the door. She frowned at him, but he merely tightened his grip.

"If we're going to be moving fast—"

"You need the support" she finished for him. "This is ridiculous. Why won't you use a cane?"

He didn't answer her because the answer was obvious. A cane meant he was no longer a whole man. A cane meant giving up and giving in. He wasn't a quitter. Never had been, never would be. "What if I told you I'm happy for any excuse to put my arm around you?"

She laughed, and he felt his body tighten in response to the enchanting sound.

"I've never met anyone so . . ."

"Honest?" he supplied.

"Blunt," she corrected. "It's disconcerting."

"No one bothers to tell you the truth?"

She raised a brow. "I'm beginning to wonder." Her gaze remained focused on her aunt and her cousin as they headed for the door to the ballroom. She led the way, moving fast enough that Joe's leg protested by amping up the pain. He gritted his teeth and kept moving.

They both came to a jolting stop when a tall man with silver threads in his black hair stepped right in front of her so abruptly that she ran right into him.

Joe grabbed Lydia possessively around the waist and glowered at the intruder. "Back off."

The man looked shocked for a moment, then surveyed Joe keenly with a gaze as cold as polar ice.

"Daddy! What are you doing here?"

Joe resisted the impulse to release his prize. This imposing man was Lydia's father? How had he found them? What did he want?

Joe had faced down generals in the past, and Bull Benedict certainly gave an equal impression of authority. He hadn't expected this complication, but he knew the best way to handle a threat was to face it head on. He squared his shoulders and stood his ground.

Joe's sister had told him that Bull Benedict was a billionaire, and he'd formed an unflattering mental image of the powerful man. To his surprise, when he surveyed Lydia's father, he saw confidence without arrogance. Joe also noticed the sudden gentleness in Bull's eyes as he looked down at his daughter.

Lydia was trembling, and Joe put his other hand around her

so she was completely enveloped in what he hoped was a reassuring embrace. She laid her hands on his where they crossed at her waist, and for a moment he thought she meant to free herself. Instead, she relaxed her body back against his, so they were aligned from chest to hips. Despite the presence of her father, Joe could feel himself becoming aroused. He muttered an oath and imagined blood and guts, anything to take away his body's unruly reaction to the woman in his arms.

"I'm here because I was worried about you," her father replied at last.

"As you can see, I'm perfectly fine," Lydia replied.

"Who is this . . . gentleman?"

Joe wondered about the pause, but figured one rogue had recognized another. He held out his right hand and said, "Joe Warren."

Bull took his hand with a firm grip and said, "Who the hell are you?"

Joe was all set to tell Bull that he was an investigator when Lydia interjected, "My date."

Bull frowned. "I thought you just turned down Harold's proposal."

"I did," Lydia said.

"And you've already got another fish on the hook?"

"Please, Daddy!" Lydia said. "You're embarrassing Joe."

Bull shot a look at Lydia's waist, which was surrounded again by both of Joe's arms, then met Joe's gaze and said, "You seem to have made yourself right at home."

Joe saw the flush rise on Lydia's neck and felt his own ears turn red. "Actually, Lydia's being kind enough to provide support. I've got a bum leg." When Bull raised a surprised brow, Joe continued, "War wound."

"You're a soldier?"

"Was one," Joe replied. "I'm no longer fit for duty." Joe heard the bitterness in his voice. He knew Lydia had detected it, because she gripped his arm more tightly, offering support he hadn't expected but found surprisingly welcome.

"What are you doing in Rome with my daughter?" Bull asked.

Joe wasn't sure whether to tell him the truth or make up a lie. Bull hadn't revealed to Lydia that he knew the Ghost had been stolen. So why was he here? It dawned on Joe that the man might simply be worried about his daughter. "I'm here from Warren and Warren Investigations to help Lydia hunt for your wife's necklace, the one that's gone missing, the one being ransomed for twenty-five million dollars."

Bull exhaled. "I see."

Joe felt Lydia turn to stone in his arms and waited along with her to see how Bull would react to the fact that Lydia had lied to him about having the Ghost in her possession.

Bull merely said, "Have you had any luck?"

Joe felt the tension leave Lydia's body as she realized that her father wasn't going to condemn her in front of him for losing the Ghost.

"Gabe stole it," Lydia blurted. "I think Aunt Alicia was in

on the theft."

Bull frowned at the suggestion that his sister-in-law had helped steal the jewel, but he didn't look shocked, which surprised Joe. Bella's sister Alicia and her son must be pretty unscrupulous characters for Bull to believe they were capable of such a daring theft.

"Let's find a place where we can talk in private," Bull said, automatically turning his head away as a flashbulb went off near them. He stopped dead in his tracks when he glanced back and saw whose photograph had just been taken.

"What the hell are you doing here?" Bull demanded.

Joe shot an inquiring look at Lydia and asked, "Who is that?"

Lydia's face blanched. "My mother."

Joe saw where Lydia had gotten her good looks. The Duchess still possessed breathtaking beauty. She was dressed in something red that emphasized a stunning figure. She was clearly startled to find Bull in the same ballroom.

"I thought you were in Paris," she said to Bull as she took the few steps to close the distance between them.

"I thought you were in Greece," he replied.

The Duchess let out a shuddering breath.

"Your Grace? May I be of assistance?"

When a woman behind the Duchess spoke, Joe suddenly noticed that Lydia's mother was being trailed by a plain woman dressed in an equally plain brown evening gown.

"I'm fine, Emily," the Duchess said.

Another flashbulb went off, lighting up both Bull and Bella.

"Let's get out of here," Bull said, taking Bella's arm and heading for the door. He glanced over his shoulder at Joe and Lydia and ordered, "Follow me."

The flashes dogged them all the way out to the limousine that was waiting at the curb. Bull helped Bella inside, then waited for Emily, Lydia, and Joe to get in before he joined everyone inside.

"Where shall I take you, sir?" the driver asked.

"Back to my hotel," Bull replied. He turned to Bella and asked more calmly, "What are you doing here?"

"I suspect I'm here for the same reason you are," Bella replied. She focused her gaze on Lydia, then shifted it to Joe. "According to my investigator, it appears my sister and her son have stolen the Ghost."

In the flickering light coming from the street lamps, Joe saw Lydia's face looked stricken.

"I'm sorry, Mother."

"I'll deal with you later," Bella said in a firm voice. She turned to Joe and said, "Your assistant called me and suggested it might behoove me to speak directly to my sister about the theft, rather than let this go on any longer."

"She called me, as well," Bull interjected. "She said it might be useful for me to be there when you confront Alicia and Gabe, since the ransom demand was sent to me."

Joe couldn't believe his sister had manipulated the situation to involve Lydia's parents without filling him in. Then he realized he'd set his phone on silent and hadn't checked it recently. He pulled it out and saw there had been numerous calls—and texts—from his sister.

"Who are you?" the Duchess said. "You're not Sam Warren. Sam Warren is the father of a grown daughter."

So, the jig was up. Poor Samantha. He hoped the Duchess wasn't going to withdraw her business from the firm. "My name is Joe Warren, ma'am. Sam Warren was my father."

"Was?" the Duchess said.

"He's been missing for two years."

To give her credit, the Duchess didn't look too perturbed when she asked, "Then who have I been corresponding with all this time?"

"My sister Samantha. She was trained by my father, which is why she's so good at what she does. She's the reason you know who stole the Ghost. I'm only here as a body in place."

He felt Lydia pinch him hard at the waist and barely managed to avoid yelping.

"Why do you suppose your sister—Samantha, is it?— invited both Bull and me to come here. She must have known I'd discover the truth about her father's absence."

"I guess she figures this is the best way to recover the Ghost, ma'am."

"Do we know where Alicia and Gabe are now?" Bella asked.

"They left the gala just before you arrived. I'd have to

check with Sam—my sister—to see if she knows where Alicia is staying."

"Do it," Bull said.

"I can't believe you lied to me," Lydia whispered to him as he made the call to Sam.

He wanted to take her in his arms and soothe the hurt look in her eyes. But that was impossible with her parents sitting across from them. "I didn't have any choice," he said.

"You always have a choice," she said. "And you made the wrong one."

She turned her head away, and Joe felt a sinking feeling in his gut. Whatever magical thing had been happening between them was over. She was cutting him out. Just as well. In a short while, Bull and Bella would confront the aunt and the cousin and this whole mess would get resolved. Then he could go home and gladly forget all about Lydia Benedict.

So why did he have this horrible ache in his throat?

CHAPTER 16

*L*ydia felt rattled. Joe Warren had been lying to her from the first moment she'd met him. He wasn't the private investigator, his sister was. Had he actually been a soldier? Or had he acquired those impressive scars and that bad leg in some other way? She should have trusted her instincts and kept her distance from the scoundrel. She felt like the world's biggest fool!

A huge knot clogged her throat and threatened to choke her. Tears welled in her eyes, and she turned away from Joe and blinked to keep them from falling. She wasn't about to give him the satisfaction of knowing how distraught she was. Once her parents confronted Alicia and Gabe and demanded the return of the Ghost, she would put this incident behind her. Joe Warren would go back to Texas, and she would go on with her life.

Lydia sniffed and realized someone had stuck a handkerchief in her hand. She looked down and saw it was one of the items she'd bought for Joe. On a whim, she'd had the Egyptian cotton embroidered with his initials. She dabbed at her eyes and nose, then turned to Joe, swallowed over the painful lump in her throat, and asked, "What comes next?"

"I have no—" Joe cut himself off as he reached for his phone, which had buzzed in his pocket. He took a moment to read a text he'd received, then said to the gathered throng, "My sister, who's been providing these leads all along, found the hotel where Alicia is staying. Sam checked with the concierge, and Alicia is in her room."

"Is Gabe with her?" Lydia asked.

"The concierge wasn't sure about that," Joe said, reading more of the text.

"Give the address to my driver," her father said.

Her mother arched a questioning brow. "Are we really going to do this right now?"

"Alicia and Gabe very likely suspect we're on to them," Joe said, shooting another brief glance in Lydia's direction. "We're better off confronting them before they can come up with a buyer for the Ghost."

"That makes sense," her mother said.

Joe gave the driver an address in a much less ritzy part of Rome. Which also made sense, Lydia realized. Gabe had protested on the phone to his mother that he was entitled to some of the wealth that had been bestowed on his cousins and denied to him. She knew her mother and her aunt had been in dire financial straits before Bull Benedict had come along. She had no idea whether her mother had provided financial support to the sister from whom she'd been estranged all these years.

"Is there any chance weapons are going to be involved in this confrontation?" Joe asked.

Lydia noticed that both of her parents, who were *sitting beside each other* across from her, looked startled. The fact that they were in the same car was a miracle in itself. To her amazement, her mother reached out a hand to her father, who took it in his and covered it reassuringly with his other hand.

Lydia's stomach knotted. This harmonious picture was too good to be true. She wondered how long it would last—and how rancorous the argument would be that separated them again.

"I don't believe Alicia will have a gun with her, if that's what you mean," her mother replied. "I'm not as sure about Gabe."

Joe focused his gaze on Bella and said, "Gabe, at least, was willing to drug and kidnap your daughter to acquire the Ghost. What makes you think he'll just give it back to you?" He turned his attention to Bull and asked, "Are you planning to pay the ransom? Or part of the ransom?"

"Hell, no!" Bull replied. "Those two will be lucky if I don't have them slapped in jail."

Joe was silent for a moment, then said, "First, you'd have to prove that they stole the Ghost. Right now, we don't have a clue where it is. All the two of them have to do is say they didn't steal it, and we don't have a shred of evidence to contradict them." He lifted a skeptical brow. "So what makes you think they'll give up the Ghost without a fight?"

"What happens if we pay them to get it back?" her mother asked.

"That's not an option," her father interjected. "It would only encourage them to do something like this again. Or to hire someone to do it for them, since they'd be first on our list of suspects."

Her mother turned to Joe and said, "I presume your sister had some sort of plan when she asked me and Bull to come here, some reason to believe that our presence would convince Alicia and Gabe to return the necklace."

Joe shook his head. "I have no idea what Sam was thinking, ma'am. I'm just telling you what I would do if I were the thieves in this situation."

"Maybe we should call your sister," Lydia suggested. "Maybe there's some information she has that we don't."

Joe responded by pulling out his phone and making the call.

His sister answered the phone with the words, "Have I been fired yet?"

Joe shot a sardonic look at Lydia's mother, then said "You're on speakerphone, Sam. I'm here with Bull and the Duchess and Lydia."

There was an awful—Oh, my God, what have I done?—

silence before Sam said, "Hello, everyone."

As an afterthought, Joe added, "Oh, and the Duchess's assistant is here, too."

Lydia suddenly realized that Emily must often be overlooked. Right now, her mother's assistant was staring out the window in an apparent effort not to intrude in a situation from which she couldn't physically remove herself.

"I'm sorry I had to lie to you, Duchess," Sam said. She continued in a single breath, "But my father disappeared from his boat off the coast of Greece two years ago, and I've finally found a lead. I needed the work you provided to finance my trip to Greece to follow that lead."

"We will discuss your future employment at another time, young lady," the Duchess said briskly. "Right now, I'm wondering if you have some plan in mind for retrieving the Ghost that's more involved than simply having Bull and me confront Alicia and Gabe. Your brother has pointed out that we have no proof they took the necklace."

"Actually," Sam began, "there is proof—in the form of emails between Gabe and potential buyers. However, I presume you don't want to resolve this issue in court."

Bella exchanged a glance with Bull, who replied, "You're correct. We'd rather keep this private."

"I believe this particular theft was a crime of opportunity on Gabe's part," Sam continued. "However, Alicia and Gabe, as a team, have been stealing jewels at charity events and selling them throughout Europe and South America for several years."

Lydia gasped in surprise. "They're actually jewel thieves?"

"I'm afraid so," Sam said.

"How do you know?" Lydia demanded. "How can you be sure?"

"It's what I do," Sam replied with alacrity.

Lydia looked at her mother, who was shaking her head in what Lydia thought might be despair. It must be awful to have a sister who'd sunk so low, even if you'd cut all ties with her years ago. But maybe it was cutting those ties that had contributed to the situation in which Aunt Alicia found herself. Could her mother possibly be blaming herself for any of this?

"So what lever are we supposed to use on those two so they'll return the Ghost?" Bella asked at last.

"Even the threat of exposing them as the thieves who took the Ghost would put them under scrutiny for a lot of jewel thefts in the past. It would also be likely to prevent them from continuing to steal without becoming suspects in future robberies. That's why I believe that simply letting them know that you know what they've been up to will cause them to cough up the necklace."

"That could work," Bella mused, exchanging a glance with Bull.

"There's one other thing you should know," Sam said.

"What's that?" Bella asked.

"Alicia didn't have anything to do with stealing the Ghost. It was all Gabe's idea. The instant she realized what Gabe had done, she tried to get him to return the necklace. I believe that, if they're confronted together, she will put pressure on her son to return the necklace."

"So they return the Ghost and then just walk away without any consequences for what Gabe did to me?" Lydia asked. "Not to mention any recompense to the owners of all the jewels they've stolen in the past—and with nothing to keep them from continuing to steal in the future?"

"That's about the size of it," Sam admitted. "Unless you want to make a Federal case out of it. Make that an Interpol case," she amended.

"Some of this may be my fault," the Duchess said. "I should have made amends with Alicia long before this." She squeezed Bull's hand. "We certainly have to the means to ease her lot. It's just that . . . I haven't been able . . . to forgive her for . . ."

As Lydia watched, her mother gripped her father's hand tighter. Her eyes were bright with tears, and she was having trouble catching her breath.

Bull put an arm around her shoulders and asked anxiously, "Bella? Are you all right?"

"Emily," the Duchess said, still breathing erratically. "My pills."

Lydia's gaze shot to Emily, who was reaching into her small clutch. She pulled out a prescription bottle of pills, poured two into her palm, and held them out to Bella.

Bull had already poured sparkling water from a bottle

he'd taken from the limousine bar into a glass and handed it to Bella.

Lydia's heart was in her throat as she watched her mother swallow the pills and then hand the crystal glass back to her father. She wanted to ask if her mother was sick, but the answer seemed obvious. Yes. She was. But what, exactly, was wrong with her?

It felt to Lydia as though everyone in the car held their collective breaths, waiting for Bella's ragged breathing to return to normal. At last, she took a deeper breath, and then another, and finally she was breathing normally again.

Lydia exhaled the breath she'd been holding in a whoosh of relief.

"Thank God," her father muttered under his breath. And then, from between clenched teeth, he said, "Don't tell me this is another panic attack. What the hell is wrong with you?"

Lydia stared at her father in confusion. *Panic attack?* She turned her gaze to her mother to see how she would answer.

"There's nothing wrong—"

"Don't give me that bullshit!" her father interrupted. "Tell me what's wrong."

Bella breathing was already more erratic as she answered, "I'm recovering . . . from the flu."

Bull grabbed her by the arms. "By God, Bella, if you don't—"

"It's her heart."

The words silenced Bull, who turned to stare at their

source—her mother's nearly-forgotten assistant.

"I'm sorry, Your Grace," Emily said. "Your condition is too fragile for such behavior."

Bull let go of Bella as though she'd caught fire. "I would never harm my wife."

"But you might kill her if you agitate her further," Emily said in a calm voice.

Her father frowned in consternation. "Bella? What is she talking about? What's wrong with you?"

Her mother took a halting breath and let it out. "I didn't want you to know. Not yet."

"Know what?" her father demanded.

"My heart is . . . damaged."

Lydia stared at her mother, her heart in her throat. "How did this happen? Can it be fixed?"

"Skiing accident," her mother replied. "My heart works fine . . . with medication. I just have to take care of myself."

"If a little argument with me upsets you this much, and causes you this much discomfort, how the hell were you planning to stay calm enough to talk Alicia into returning the Ghost?" Bull said angrily.

"I don't intend to let Alicia provoke me," Bella said with a smile.

"What doctors have you seen?" Bull asked.

"I've seen the best doctors to be found," Bella said. "Please, Bull. I don't want to discuss this. There's nothing anyone can do."

"Are you dying?" Lydia hadn't meant to blurt the question, but she wanted to know just how sick her mother was.

Her mother's smile widened. "Of course not! I just have to take my medication and take it easy."

"Are you sure you should talk to Aunt Alicia?" Lydia asked. "What if she starts shouting at you? What if she makes a terrible scene?"

Bella made a *tsking* sound and looked from Lydia to Bull and back to Lydia again. "This is why I didn't want anyone to know about my heart being injured. I'm not an invalid. Please don't treat me like one."

Lydia shot a look at Emily to see whether her mother's assistant agreed with Bella's assessment of her heart condition, but Emily was staring out the window. Lydia felt Joe squeeze her hand and wondered when she'd reached out to him. She felt cold inside, and the warmth of his hand was reassuring.

This situation was all her fault. If she hadn't borrowed the Ghost without permission, it would be safe in the vault at Blackthorne Abbey right now. Her mother wouldn't be risking her life—or at least the possibility of a heart attack—in order to get it back. Lydia felt horribly guilty. She would never forgive herself if anything happened to the Duchess.

As of today, Lydia vowed, she was turning over a new leaf. She was going to grow up and act responsibly, instead of like a selfish child. That meant not playing around with Joe Warren. She eased her fingers free of his grasp. He gave her a questioning look but let her go.

Lydia felt a sinking feeling in her stomach. She didn't want to say goodbye to Joe. But if she was going to do the grownup thing, she had to start treating him like the "body in place" he'd said he was, nothing more, nothing less. She eased her thigh away from the heat of his, smoothing her skirt down along her leg to separate them more completely.

She felt him stiffen beside her and knew he was aware of her withdrawal.

Before he could speak, the driver announced, "We're here."

CHAPTER 17

*J*oe was pretty sure the Duchess was lying about the severity of her heart condition. Before her assistant had passed her those pills, her complexion had turned a pasty gray—a clear sign that her heart wasn't providing enough oxygen to keep her alive. He wasn't surprised that Lydia and her father had swallowed the lie. That was easier than believing that the life of such a vibrant mother and wife might be cut short.

More troubling to him was the way Lydia had separated herself so completely from him. When she'd reached for his hand, he'd been more than glad to provide comfort. He wondered if she'd suddenly realized that she was holding his hand in full view of her parents, or whether there was some other reason she'd pulled away.

Once Joe was out of the limo, he held out a hand to Lydia, but she avoided his offer of help and got out on her own. He frowned and followed her up the steps to the front door of the hotel.

"Which room?" Bull asked Joe as he escorted Bella and her assistant inside.

"She's on the first floor," Joe replied. "Room 110."

When they reached the room, Bull knocked loudly on the door. When it remained unanswered, he called out, "Alicia, we know you're in there. Open the damn door!"

Joe was surprised at how frazzled Alicia looked as she released the chain and opened the door.

She said, "Come in," and stepped back to allow everyone to enter, letting the door slide closed behind them. She hadn't changed out of her ballgown, but she'd let her hair down. Joe thought it made her look a lot more like the Duchess.

Joe looked immediately for Gabe and spied him sitting in a chair in the corner of the room. A gentleman would have risen at the entrance of two ladies, one of whom was his aunt, but Gabe gripped the arms of the upholstered chair as though it—or he—might fly away if he let go.

Joe was instantly wary, recognizing the signs of suppressed rage in Gabe's tightly clenched jaw and the tense set of his shoulders. He put himself between Gabe and the women while he waited for whatever came next.

"You know why we're here?" the Duchess said to her sister.

Alicia nodded abruptly without admitting anything.

Bull was more direct. He turned to Gabe and said, "The jig is up, boy. Hand it over. Now."

Gabe's eyes looked wild, and he hunkered into the chair like a treed wildcat, his fingernails digging into the chair like claws, as he growled, "I have no idea what you're talking about."

Alicia made a dying sound in her throat. "Give him the necklace, Gabe. Please."

"I want it back," Lydia said, crossing past Joe before he could catch her and holding out a waiting hand under her cousin's nose.

"Go away, brat," Gabe said.

Joe saw Lydia draw back as though she'd been slapped. She hadn't expected to be called "brat." It sounded like something her brothers—and her cousin—might have said to get rid of her when she was a kid who wanted to join in. Joe caught her around the waist as she reached out to grab a handful of Gabe's hair. "Whoa, there!"

She turned on Joe as though he were the villain, pounding on the arm that held her captive. "Let me go!"

"Settle down," he said in the commanding voice he'd used as a soldier when he gave an order he expected to be obeyed.

It didn't work on Lydia. "Put me down," she insisted, kicking him in his bad leg.

Joe grunted at the pain, which seared its way from his knee downward through his devastated calf.

Lydia froze for a moment and looked up at him. "I'm sorry. I didn't mean to hurt you."

Joe hadn't realized he'd lifted her completely off the floor, but it felt like his bad leg was ready to collapse, so he set her on her feet. She turned within the stricture of his arm, put her hands on his chest, and said, "I'm so sorry. But you shouldn't have tried to stop me."

"I wasn't sure what he might do," Joe said through teeth clenched against the pain. "I didn't want you to get hurt."

Gabe suddenly rose from his chair and faced the crowd like a trapped animal, desperate to escape. He focused his anger on Bull and said, "I deserve more than you've given me. I should have—"

"Gabe, no!" Alicia cried. "Don't, please. I beg you."

Joe felt Lydia freeze in his grasp as she directed her attention toward the play being enacted before her.

Joe watched as Gabe visibly gathered his composure. Alicia's son shot a nasty look at Bull, who frowned, then looked at Alicia, and paled. So. It was true. Bull just might be the boy's father. For some reason, Alicia didn't want the truth out in the open. All of them had backed off rather than confront the potentially life-altering issue.

Gabe slowly reached inside his tux pants pocket and pulled out a black velvet bag, which he tossed at Lydia. Joe caught it before it could strike her in the head and then dropped it into her outstretched hand.

"Why, you—" Bull began, when it seemed apparent that Gabe had meant to hit Lydia with the necklace.

Bella caught his arm to keep him from throwing a punch and said, "No, Bull. We have the necklace. That's enough."

"Is that what's in the bag?" Joe asked. He wouldn't have put it past Gabe to put something else in there.

Lydia quickly opened the drawstring and withdrew the Ghost.

Joe was hard-pressed to keep from gasping at the array of sapphires, rubies, emeralds, and diamonds that sparkled around the enormous drop pearl. He'd never seen anything so beautiful—or so priceless—not counting the flesh-and-blood woman in his arms.

Lydia left his embrace and crossed the room to hand the necklace to her mother. "Here it is, Mother. I'm so sorry I took it without asking."

"Are you sure it isn't paste?" Joe asked, still unsure to what lengths Gabe might be willing to go to steal the Ghost.

Lydia's mother examined the necklace and said, "It's real."

"How do you know?" Joe asked, truly curious how she could tell the real thing from something fake.

"By this." She held out the necklace to him, and Joe leaned over to look at what she was pointing out.

"What am I looking at?" he asked.

"The chip in this sapphire." Bella glanced at Bull, and Joe thought she blushed as she said, "I dropped the necklace the same day it was given to me and chipped this stone."

"I never noticed that," Lydia said. "Why didn't you have the chipped stone replaced?"

"Because . . ." Bella met Bull's gaze and finished, "I never wanted to forget what your father and I shared that day."

This time it was Bull's cheeks that looked pink. Joe wasn't a mind reader, but he had a feeling Bella might have expressed her appreciation to Bull for the necklace in some way that had resulted in the necklace becoming unimportant enough to end up getting dropped on the floor.

"What now?" Alicia asked, her eyes frightened and her body trembling.

"Now we all go home," Bella said.

"Easy for you to say," Alicia retorted, as fear mush-roomed into rage. "You have Blackthorne Abbey." She shot a narrow-eyed look in Bull's direction. "And his billions." She turned her furious gaze back on Bella as she finished, "Gabe and I share a small flat in London. We have to live by our wits—"

"And by stealing," Bella interrupted.

"You can't blame us for doing what we have to do to survive," Alicia said. "It's not fair that you should have every-thing and we should have nothing. You should have shared, Bella. A loving sister—"

"How dare you!" Bella said in a steely voice. "I was willing to share everything. That changed because of your behavior. You know what you did."

Joe was lost. Something had obviously happened to alienate the sisters from each other, but it was impossible to tell from what Bella had said exactly what it was Alicia had done.

"Bella," Bull said. "That's enough."

Joe realized the Duchess's breathing had become erratic again.

"Your Grace!" her assistant said urgently. "You must

calm yourself."

Alicia looked confused by Bella's behavior. "Bella? What's wrong?"

"We're leaving," Bull said, ushering Bella toward the door.

"Goodbye and good riddance," Gabe called after them.

Once they were outside the room with the door closed behind them, Bull lifted Bella into his arms.

"That's not necessary," Bella said.

"When I hear your breathing return to normal, I'll set you down," Bull said brusquely.

He was still carrying her when they reached the front door of the hotel.

"This is where we part ways," Joe said to Lydia's parents as the limo pulled up to the curb. "I'm sure my sister will be in touch."

"Don't you want a ride back to your hotel?" Bella asked.

Joe shot a glance at Lydia. He didn't have a room of his own. He'd been sharing hers. "No thanks. I can manage on my own."

To his surprise, Lydia said, "I have a few things to discuss with Joe before he leaves. I'll go with him."

Lydia's father had set Bella on her feet, and Lydia hugged her mother goodbye. "Please say you forgive me, Mother."

"I think you've learned your lesson," the Duchess replied.

"Come here, sweetheart," her father said, gathering her in his arms and hugging her close. "Be good." He glanced over her shoulder and met Joe's eyes as he added, "And if you can't be good, be careful."

Joe felt the tips of his ears redden again. He supposed it didn't take much divining by her father to figure out that he was as susceptible to Lydia Benedict's siren call as any other man. He was sorry their interlude was over. Somehow, in just two days, he'd fallen under her spell. He wasn't sorry their paths had crossed, but the sooner he got out of here, the less heartache he would have to endure.

Lydia stood beside him and waved as her parents' limo drove away. Then she turned to him and said, "We need to talk."

CHAPTER 18

*B*ella invited Bull into her suite, then spoke privately for a moment with Emily before her assistant retired to her own room.

As the door to the suite closed behind the young woman, Bull said, "She didn't look like she wanted to leave you alone."

"Emily worries about me."

"It seems like she has good reason to be concerned," Bull said as he crossed to stand in front of her. "Just how sick are you, Bella? This time I want the truth."

Bella kept her features even and worked hard to stay relaxed, so her pulse would remain under control. "Why don't we sit down?"

He took her by the shoulders and pulled her so close she could see the black irises within his blue eyes grow large as he drank in the sight of her. She was aware of the heat of him and the familiar masculine smell that was his alone. It had been so long! She wanted to wrap her arms around him and never let go. But she remained still, not wanting to encourage Bull to take the embrace further. At least, not before they'd talked about the tragedy that had separated them.

"I've spent ten miserable years without you," he said in a low, hoarse voice. "Tell me that you're going to be okay. Tell me that we have a lifetime ahead of us."

Just being close to Bull was exhilarating. She laid her head against his chest so she could feel the beat of his powerful heart and put her arms around his waist. She should have made peace with him years ago. She hadn't been any happier without him than he'd apparently been without her.

But she'd been fuming mad when he'd accused her of cheating on him with another man. She'd become frantic and desperate as the stubborn man refused to listen when, at last, she'd tried to defend herself. She'd ended up offended—and unforgiving—because he'd trusted her so little that he'd actually believed she'd broken her wedding vows.

And, of course, she'd thought they had forever to make amends. The fact that they didn't made it easier to say the quiet words she spoke next.

"It wasn't me that you saw in our bed with another man. It was Alicia."

"Alicia?" Bull jerked away and stared at her in horror. "Why didn't you just say so ten years ago?"

Bella sighed and sank onto the closest surface, which

happened to be the sofa. "You never gave me the chance."

"You could have made me listen," he said furiously. "Why didn't you?"

"I was appalled—and hurt—that you could believe I would betray you like that."

"What on earth was she doing in our bed?" Bull said.

Bella sighed. That was a much longer story, which she had no intention of telling Bull right now. Instead, she shrugged and said, "Who knows? Some crazy whim of hers, I suppose."

He sank onto the sofa beside her. "God, Bella. What a fool I've been." He shoved both hands through his hair, leaving it askew. He met her gaze, a deep, vertical furrow appearing between his brows, and said, "What fools we've both been."

Bella couldn't disagree. They'd lost ten years that they could have spent loving each other. Ten years that they couldn't get back. And she didn't dare spend time with Bull now, or he would discover the truth about her precarious health. If he did, he would surely try to stop her from accomplishing the goal she'd set for herself before she died: finding loving partners for her unmarried children.

She felt a niggling dissatisfaction and wondered at its source, until Bull sighed heavily and said, "I'm sorry, Bella. I should have trusted you. I shouldn't have gone off half-cocked like that. I should have believed in our love. Can you forgive me?"

There it was. The apology that provided a healing balm

to the terrible ache in her heart. Bull's admission that the love they'd shared should have been enough to convince him his eyes had deceived him. That he couldn't possibly have seen his wife in bed with another man, because she'd loved him too much ever to dishonor him—or their love—in such a manner.

Bella suddenly felt like she could run forever, the wind in her hair, her arms held wide in exultation. But considering the state of her heart, she was happy to settle for making love to her husband. She'd missed being held in Bull's arms. Tonight she intended to make up for lost time.

She rose, reached out a hand to him, smiled sweetly and said, "Come with me."

Despite the impression she'd given to her husband, Bella had been faithful to her marriage vows. She had no idea whether the same was true of Bull. She didn't ask, because she didn't want to know if he'd found release in another woman's body. After all, his wife had rejected him and made it plain that she wanted nothing to do with him. If he'd been unfaithful, it was because she'd sent him away.

"You're every bit as beautiful as I remembered," Bull said in a reverent voice as he eased her evening gown off her shoulders. Bella shivered with excitement as he placed a kiss on the flesh he'd bared.

They undressed each other impatiently, Bull shoving at her dress to get it out of his way, while Bella pushed his tuxedo jacket off his shoulders. She reached for the studs in his shirt, tossing them aside as though they were glass, rather than the expensive diamonds they were. She was laughing, giddy with joy as they stripped their clothes away, until at last they stood across from one another, as naked as Adam and Eve in the Garden of Eden.

Bella let her eyes roam what she desired and noticed the subtle changes that ten years had wrought in Bull's body. His shoulders were still broad and muscular, and his waist was still trim, but the crow's feet around his eyes had grown deeper, and the black curls on his chest were now threaded with silver. She didn't have to wonder whether he still desired her. Her eyes trailed down his flat belly to the erection that throbbed in expectation of their joining.

She resisted the urge to cover her body as his eyes roamed over her the way hers had over him. Her breasts were not as high as they'd once been, and her belly was not as flat, despite all the yoga and pilates she'd done. And where gray had sprouted at Bull's temples and on his chest, she had silver among the black curls that protected her womanhood.

They had both grown older. And hopefully wiser. She, at least, had realized that life was finite, and that it should be grasped with both hands and lived to the fullest. She smiled to herself, certain that her doctor would approve of the moderate exercise she had in mind over the next hour or so.

They came together slowly, electricity arcing between them and sending frissons of feeling up and down Bella's spine. She savored the feel of her breasts nestled in the rough hair on

Bull's chest, the feel of his warmth and heat and hardness against her thigh as his arms closed tightly around her.

Bella realized she was trembling as Bull's lips touched hers, tasting, looking for differences, then capturing her mouth and taking what he wanted. The familiar blended with the strange to create unimaginable pleasure. Overlaying it all was the sheer thrill of knowing they were together once again.

She gave a giddy laugh when he picked her up and headed for the bedroom. He set her down long enough to tear the covers from the bed, and she heard a guttural moan of pleasure issue from her lips as he lowered her to the sheets and covered her body with his own.

He felt so good. So right.

"I want you," he said in a harsh voice.

She couldn't wait either. They'd been apart too long to want to play. She needed to be joined with him. *Now. I need you inside me. Please, Bull.* She reached for him and guided him home.

She cried out as he plunged to the hilt, and he stopped and would have pulled out, except that she wrapped her legs around him to keep him inside. "I'm okay," she rasped. "It's just . . . It's been a long time for me."

"How long?"

There was no help for it. She would have to tell him the truth. "Ten years."

Bull groaned, a rough, animal sound. He put his hands to either side of her face and kissed her, thrusting his tongue deep to claim her. Then he looked deep into her eyes and said, "My beautiful wife."

He didn't admit to similar celibacy. She hadn't expected it, and she didn't blame him for it. But she was glad that he treasured her fidelity. And she was glad they were going to have this moment in time to enjoy the pleasures of the flesh that she'd missed over the years they'd been apart.

He was as gentle as a man ravenous for a woman could be. Bella found herself smiling as her husband moved heaven and earth to bring her to fulfillment. His climax came before hers, but he knew enough to make certain she found the same joy in their coupling. When it finally happened, her release was earth-shattering.

All through their lovemaking, Bella had been unaware of her heart. It wasn't until they were lying together, lungs heaving, bodies slick with sweat, that she realized her heart was thundering in her chest. And it hurt.

She put a palm against her chest as though she could will her heart to slow, and then she concentrated on the mountain lake that was the place of peace she always imagined when she wanted to calm herself.

"Bella?"

She heard the concern in Bull's voice, but she wasn't sure what was causing it. Then she realized he'd raised himself up on an elbow and was looking down at her with those beautiful, piercing blue eyes. He must have asked her a question or something that she hadn't answered. She closed her eyes and concentrated on breathing in and out, in and out.

"Bella!"

She opened her eyes and tried to smile, but her lips wobbled. "I'm fine." The words came out in a whisper and wouldn't have convinced anyone, let alone an anxious husband, that she was as fine as she'd claimed to be.

"I'm going to call a doctor."

She reached out and caught his arm before he could leave the bed. She spoke a careful, single word at a time. "I. Will. Be. Fine."

He took her in his arms and held her close, rocking her as though she were dying. "Don't leave me, Bella. Please, don't leave me."

"I'm not. Going. Anywhere."

He gave a weak laugh and said, "You got two words together that time."

She managed to smile back. "I need to. Exercise. My heart. But I don't think. My doctor had. This in mind."

"You should have told me. I wouldn't have—"

She laid her fingertips against his lips to silence him. Her heart rate was slowing, and she could feel the strength flowing back into her limbs and her lungs. She took a deeper breath and let it out, and then another. She smiled at him and said, "I'm better already."

"This is ridiculous. I'm going to take you to a specialist."

"I've been to a specialist," she said, her voice almost back to normal. "I just need rest." She smiled invitingly.

"And exercise."

"No," Bull said, pulling her into his lap and holding her close. "Not again. Not until you're well."

That wasn't going to work because she was never going to be well. Bella knew better than to argue with him. She'd never met a man as stubborn as Bull Benedict. Instead, she slid her arms around his neck and said, "Whatever you say, Bull."

He tightened his arms around her. "Damn straight."

Bella suppressed a girlish giggle. Despite her husband's honorable protestations, she could feel his arousal grow and throb beneath her. They had a long night ahead of them. With any luck, it wouldn't take much persuasion to change his mind.

Tomorrow morning she would explain that she had business in Greece and had to get back. In fact, she had to find a wife for Riley. Bella froze as she realized the solution to her problem might have been right under her nose all along.

Samantha Warren needed to spend time in Greece hunting for her missing father. Bella had actually met the girl when she was younger, and she'd promised to be quite a beauty. Who better to help Sam find her father than Bella's son Riley, who was completely at home on the ocean? Bella realized that she could invite Sam to come to Greece on the pretext of discussing her future employment as the investigator for the Duchess of Blackthorne. She would make sure Riley was on hand and heard about Sam's need to find her father. What red-blooded male could resist helping a female in distress?

Once she'd introduced the two of them, all she had to do was let nature take its course.

As it had with Sam's brother Joe and the Duchess's wayward daughter. Joe had come to Lydia's aid and managed to charm her in record time. If Bella wasn't mistaken, the two of them were well on their way to making a match. When they did, she would present the Ghost to her daughter as a wedding gift. After all, it was what had brought them together in the first place.

Satisfied that she'd settled matters to her satisfaction, the Duchess turned her attention to seducing her husband. She slid her fingers into the hair at Bull's nape and felt him shiver. She pressed his head down so their lips could meet and slid her tongue into his mouth.

After that, she let nature take its course.

CHAPTER 19

*E*ver since he'd talked with Lydia on the phone, Oliver hadn't been able to stop thinking about his younger sister, wondering if she was in trouble. Getting a text from Bull was odd enough that it signaled something was afoot. He needed to know that Lydia was all right, and that she'd actually had his mother's permission to borrow the Ghost. And the best way to find out the truth was to check out the situation himself.

Rather than confront Lydia directly, which might suggest that he didn't trust her, he'd decided it would be better to ask questions of his mother's able assistant. He'd met Emily Sheldon on several occasions, and she'd struck him as a very capable woman. She would be likely to know more about what was going on than anyone else. Moreover, she could be trusted to be discreet about the fact that he'd been making inquiries.

The techniques Oliver employed that helped him to locate missing art were useful in helping him to locate his mother and her assistant. To his surprise, it turned out they were in Rome. That was suspicious, because the last time he'd checked, his mother was in Greece. So why had she left and gone to Rome? What the hell was going on with that necklace?

Within an hour of his arrival in Rome, Oliver knocked on the hotel room door where his mother's assistant was staying. He was shaken, because when he'd inquired at the front desk, he'd discovered that a gentleman matching his father's description had arrived with his mother much earlier in the evening—and hadn't yet left.

He couldn't imagine what his father was doing in Rome, especially in the company of his mother, but it made him even more concerned about what kind of trouble his little sister had gotten herself into.

Emily Sheldon answered his knock wearing a full-length, faded-pink cotton robe. Her face was devoid of makeup, revealing a face that was saved from being completely forgettable by a pair of inquisitive brown eyes. She'd tied her brown hair up in a messy knot on the top of her head, but numerous curls had escaped and floated around her face, softening an angular jaw and square cheekbones.

He amended his earlier judgment about her forgettable features when she opened her mouth to speak. His eyes locked on her lips, which were bowed at the top and full at the bottom. It was a mouth made for kissing, although he doubted it had been used for that purpose anytime in the recent past. Quite frankly, Miss Sheldon was the most off-putting female he'd ever met. Her rigid posture, her frank stare, and her firm jaw didn't encourage familiarity.

She leaned forward and looked left and right down the empty hallway, then said, "How may I help you, milord?"

"For a start, stop 'milording' me," he said irritably. "And invite me in, so we can have this conversation in private."

She flushed, but her chin came up, and she said, "If you will wait downstairs, I will dress and meet you—"

He stepped past her into the room and shut the door behind him. "Dressing would be pointless. I've already seen you in your robe and without your makeup."

He knew she was annoyed, even though her face stayed expressionless, because those vibrant brown eyes of hers were flashing death and destruction in his direction.

She tightened the tie at her waist, which caused him to realize just how small a span it was. Then she crossed her arms over her breasts, which he could see were softly rounded, except where the budded nipples were clearly visible beneath the worn cotton.

Oliver was startled to realize that his body was responding with amazing vigor to the sight of Miss Sheldon in her robe. Maybe he should have listened to her and waited downstairs while she dressed. But he was here now, so he might as well ask his questions and get out.

"Did my sister have permission from my mother to borrow the Ghost?"

"Why do you ask?"

"Answer the question."

Her brown eyes darkened with disapproval, and she did something with her beautiful lips that made them completely disappear. "I'm not sure that's any of your business."

Oliver wasn't used to people telling him no. Despite her helpless appearance, Miss Sheldon was obviously more lion than mouse. "I came all the way to Rome from Argentina, because I'm worried about my sister," he said. "Can you just tell me what's going on with the Ghost? Is Lydia in trouble? Or not?"

He couldn't believe how long it took Miss Sheldon to decide to answer him. At last she said, "Lydia never got permission from the Duchess to borrow the Ghost."

"Son of a bitch!"

She shot him an admonishing look and continued, "She was drugged and the Ghost was stolen from her."

"Bloody hell," he muttered. "Is she all right?

She frowned ferociously. "Swear again, and I won't bother to finish this story."

He balled his hands into fists at his sides, but he shut his mouth and listened.

"Except for being drugged, Lydia wasn't harmed," she said. "The Duchess contacted Warren and Warren Investigations, a firm in Dallas, Texas, and they sent Joe Warren to Rome to help Lydia discover who'd taken the necklace."

Miss Sheldon looked around as though seeking a place to sit. Her room contained only a bed, a desk, and a lounge chair. Given those three options, she remained standing.

Oliver resisted the urge to insert another question, and waited impatiently for her to continue.

She shoved a stray curl away from her neck, and he found himself admiring her swanlike throat. When he met her gaze again, he saw that she'd followed the direction of his gaze and was frowning at him again. There was nothing bland about Miss Sheldon when she was frowning.

"It turned out that your cousin, Gabriel Wharton, was the one who drugged Lydia and stole the Ghost," she said. "Apparently, he and his mother have been stealing jewels at charity events for quite some time."

Oliver bit his tongue to prevent another foul epithet from escaping.

"The private investigator suggested that the best way to get the Ghost back was for your mother and father to confront your cousin and your aunt and demand the return of the necklace."

"Did that work?" Oliver asked incredulously.

Miss Sheldon shook her head in what seemed like disbelief equal to his own as she admitted, "I didn't think it would work, either, but it did. Gabriel returned the Ghost on the spot."

Oliver let out a relieved breath. "I suppose all's well that ends well."

"No one was punished," Miss Sheldon pointed out. "Not your sister, who borrowed the Ghost without permission, nor your cousin, who drugged your sister and stole the necklace, nor your aunt, who was complicit in the theft. That doesn't sound like a proper ending to me."

Oliver understood why his parents hadn't prosecuted his cousin. It would have created a scandal to admit that Gabe had drugged Lydia and stolen the Ghost. And surely Lydia had learned her lesson after being drugged and losing the Ghost, not to mention the anxiety of needing to find the missing necklace before its loss was discovered. But clearly, Miss Sheldon wanted each of them to experience some sort of retribution. He met her gaze and asked, "What punishment do you suggest?"

"I'm not Lydia's mother. Or Gabe's keeper. It isn't for me to say."

"But you obviously have an opinion," he persisted.

"Both of those young people need an occupation to engage their hearts and minds—and to keep their hands busy. Jewels should be the last thing on either of their minds."

"I can't say I disagree with you. However, I'm not sure how that goal can be accomplished."

"That responsibility lies with their parents," Miss Sheldon said flatly.

Oliver realized that he was amused. "Are you criticizing your employer, Miss Sheldon?"

Her ivory complexion turned as pink as her faded robe. "I was in Richmond on Mother's Day, milord."

He scowled. "I said to cut out—"

"What am I to call you?" she demanded.

"Call me Oliver. It's my name."

"Fine, *Oliver*. I was there to see the Duchess's heartbreak when not one of her five children responded to her invitation to join her in Richmond. So yes, I think she indulged the lot of you too much. To put a point on it, you're all spoiled rotten, selfish, and insensitive to the feelings of others, including your own mother."

Her expression had become as animated as her voice, and although her words stung, Oliver found himself entranced by the woman who spoke them. Still, he was unwilling to accept her assessment of him and his siblings.

"You don't know anything about me," he said in a harsh voice. "Certainly not enough to condemn me with the same broad brush you're using to condemn my brothers and sister. I haven't lived the same life as they have. And I had my reasons for not joining my mother, as I'm sure my brothers and sister did."

"It was cruel to abandon the Duchess like that," she said flatly.

"She was the one who abandoned us," Oliver shot back. He didn't owe Emily Sheldon an explanation, but he offered one anyway. "A lot happened before you came into the picture three years ago. Don't judge what you don't know."

Earnest brown eyes searched his own dark orbs before she said, "I know that adults can make choices about how they behave. I know that a person can rise above the hurts he suffered as a child. I know those things because I grew up in a family even larger than yours, with parents who were never there to provide any guidance. You can't blame your parents for the way you turned out. The responsibility is entirely your own."

He didn't appreciate the sermon, even if he agreed with a lot of what she'd said. "I'm surprised you continue to work for my mother if you think she did such a terrible job raising her kids."

"I admire your mother," she said. "She has tremendous strength of will. And she loves her children more than any of you can imagine."

"How would you know something like that, Miss Sheldon?" Oliver asked in a sharp voice.

"I've spent every day with the Duchess for the past three years," she replied. "I've been there to see your neglect of her. I've been there to see her efforts to love you all in spite of it."

Oliver felt a spurt of guilt for spending so little time with his mother and then felt angry with Emily Sheldon for making him feel bad about it. "If my mother wanted us around, she'd make more time for us. She's had other things on her mind for the past ten years."

"You'll be happy to know those days are over," Miss Sheldon replied tartly.

"What are you talking about?"

"I believe your parents have reconciled."

Oliver was startled into blurting, "What? When?"

"I left the two of them in your mother's room earlier this

evening. I asked the concierge to let me know when your father left, because I wanted to check on the Duchess. He's still there." She took a deep breath and added, "I believe he plans to stay the night."

Oliver let out a shuddering breath. His parents reunited? His parents a couple again? It seemed impossible that they could have overcome ten years of animosity in a single day.

"Why did she forgive him? How could he forgive her?"

"You would have to ask them," Miss Sheldon said. "All I know is that they were in accord when I left the room, and they've spent the better part of the evening in each other's company."

Oliver realized he'd gotten everything he'd come for. It was time for him to take his leave. "Goodbye, Miss Sheldon. I'm sorry for having inconvenienced you."

She was flushing again, which created unflattering red splotches on her peaches-and-cream English complexion. "It was no trouble."

He smiled sardonically. "I was a pain in the ass. But you won't have to worry about my bothering you again."

"But—" She cut herself off, frowned, shook her head, and pursed her lips.

"Was there something else?" he asked, arching a brow.

"Will you be coming to the Abbey for Christmas?" she asked in a rush.

"You seem to think we'll be having Christmas at the Abbey. We haven't for ten years."

"I mean, if your parents are together," she said.

"If they're together . . ." He smiled cynically. "I guess I'll believe it when I see it. *Au revoir*, Miss Sheldon."

"Goodbye, Oliver," Miss Sheldon said, her brown eyes bright with what he suddenly realized were tears. "I will hope to see you at Christmas."

He didn't look back as he left the room. He'd seen the desolation in her eyes, the certain knowledge that she was destined to spend her life alone. He recognized the look because he'd seen it so often in his own mirror. There was nothing he could do to help Miss Sheldon. As she'd said, everyone had to make choices. He'd chosen not to give anyone the power to hurt him by making himself vulnerable. So he wouldn't be looking for a woman to love—or a woman to love him.

At least the trip had been worthwhile. He'd learned everything he needed to know—and a lot more than he'd expected. Now he wanted to see Lydia, to make sure she suffered the consequences that Miss Sheldon had said would be so good for her character. He would make it plain to Lydia that she had lost his trust. And that it was going to take a very long time—and a great deal of effort on her part—to earn it back.

He looked at his watch. It was late. She was probably in bed. He shouldn't bother her. But if he talked with her now, he could refuel the jet and head right back to Argentina.

Oliver had the address of her hotel in his pocket. He might as well wake her up and read her the riot act tonight.

CHAPTER 20

"*I*'ll be out of your hair as soon as I dump this tux," Joe said as they stepped into Lydia's hotel room.

"We need to talk first," she replied, stopping just inside the room.

Joe turned to find her leaning back against the door with her arms crossed, like a schoolmarm with a disruptive pupil. He felt his neck hairs hackle. None of this was his fault. He'd been doing his sister a favor, not that he owed Miss High-and-Mighty an explanation.

Nevertheless, he was surprised, considering how reluctant he'd been to come here in the first place, how reluctant he was to leave. It was the girl, of course. She'd gotten under his skin. Right now she was pissed off because he hadn't been completely honest. He could appreciate that. But he didn't want to spend his last night in Rome fighting with her. He wanted to spend it deep inside her.

Joe felt his body responding to the memory of holding Lydia in his arms, of kissing her breasts and watching the ecstasy in her violet eyes when she came. He took the few steps to put himself body-to-body with her and watched as an invisible "No Trespassing" sign went up, warning him to keep his distance.

Joe ignored it.

"What do you think you're doing?" Lydia demanded indignantly as he slid one arm around her waist and used his free hand to angle her head for his kiss.

"Making love to you." He teased her lips open with his tongue, searching for the delicious honey inside. He made a sound of satisfaction when she thrust her hands into his hair to pull him close as her body surged against his.

She broke the kiss to gasp, "I'm still angry with you."

"I know."

"You shouldn't have lied to me."

"I did it to help my sister," he murmured against her lips.

She ran her fingernail along the edge of his ear, raising gooseflesh on his body. "I need to know I can trust you."

"Roger that. You have my word," he said, pressing kisses on the tender flesh at her throat, "that I will never lie to you again."

She quivered in his arms as she whispered, "Be sure you don't. Not ever again, so long as we both shall live."

That statement seemed to presume that he would be around for a great deal more than one more day. Joe felt a surge of joy—or something very much like it.

His body tightened as Lydia sucked on his lower lip. She made a satisfied sound in her throat as she slid her hand down between them, boldly tracing the rock-hard length of him.

Joe had never wanted a woman as much as he did in that moment. While Lydia stepped out of her very high heels, his hands got busy pulling down the zipper on her gown and urgently shoving the silk fabric out of his way. He made short work of the merry widow she was wearing, but his eyes went wide with amusement and delight when he spied the lacy garter belt that held up her black silk stockings and the ridiculous scrap of black lace between her thighs that served as feminine underwear.

"You really know how to drive a man crazy," he muttered as he slowly untied the slender strings on either side that held the panties in place. The scrap of silk and lace dangled from his fingertips for a moment before it floated to the floor. Joe had no intention of removing the stockings, since they weren't in his way.

His fingers sought the warm folds between her legs, and he stimulated the small bud he found there, while his deep, thrusting kisses mimicked the movement of his fingers.

Lydia moaned and arched her body toward him, shoving at his tuxedo jacket and pulling at the studs on his shirt in an effort to free him of the clothing that kept her naked flesh apart from his.

Joe released her long enough to shrug out of his jacket and rid himself of his shirt and cummerbund. Then he scooped her up in his arms and strode toward the bedroom.

He felt Lydia's fingernails dig into his back as she grabbed hold. Her face was level with his chest, and she leaned close enough to tease one of his nipples with her teeth.

Joe hissed in a breath, aroused by the brief, sharp pain. She immediately soothed the hurt by sucking on the nipple, and he groaned as his shaft bucked with need.

Lydia stripped the covers back as Joe settled her gently on the sheets. He could feel her gaze on him, devouring him with her eyes as he rid himself of shoes, socks, trousers, and undershorts. She held out her open arms to him, and he willingly joined her on the bed.

He would have played more, but Lydia seemed as impatient as he was to join their bodies. He made them one with a single, deep thrust and felt her legs close tightly around his hips as he sank into her to the hilt.

"Joe." She said his name as though it were a prayer of thanksgiving. She looked up at him, a plea in her eyes, and he realized he would do anything, say anything, be anything to make her happy.

His muscular arms braced his body above her as he gazed down into her remarkable violet eyes. What was she thinking at this moment? What did she feel for him? He saw desire. And longing. But for what? The simple pleasures of the flesh? Or did she yearn for something deeper, some profound emotional connection that he would have said—before he'd met Lydia Benedict—was impossible on such short acquaintance.

Their lovemaking was tender at first, but quickly escalated to urgent kisses and desperate touches. Joe had never made love to a woman who responded to him so avidly, who sought to give as much enjoyment as she took.

She stroked.

He caressed.

She bit.

He teased with his teeth.

She scratched.

He smoothed a callused palm over sensitive flesh.

She licked.

He sucked.

She moaned.

He made a guttural sound of satisfaction.

Joe waited until he felt Lydia's writhing body had reached the limits of her control. Then he shoved her over the edge and leaped off the cliff after her, catching her on the way down.

His lungs were heaving, his pulse pounding as he eased his weight off of her and spooned her against his belly. He slid an arm around her and pressed his nose against her fragrant hair.

He was almost asleep when Lydia spoke.

"What are we going to do?"

"About what?" he mumbled against her shoulder.

"About us."

It was plain that she wasn't going to let him sleep. Joe rolled over onto his back and laid an arm across his eyes. He forced himself to remember the pleasure he'd just enjoyed with her and refrained from pointing out that when a man was sated and sleepy was not the best time to engage him in conversation.

He glanced over and saw that she had also turned over onto her back and was staring up at the ceiling. He pushed himself up and rested his head on his hand so he could look down into her face, the sheer beauty of which reminded him that he was way out of his league.

"I didn't realize there *was* an us," he said.

She rolled onto her side to face him, her head on the pillow, her hands balled into fists that she tucked under her chin. She took a deep breath and said, "I don't want you to leave."

Joe wasn't entirely surprised. They'd had a good time together hunting down the Ghost. The sex was amazing. And there was just enough friction between them—due to the enormous difference in their backgrounds—to keep things interesting. She'd just rejected her would-be fiancé, so she was free to play at romance with another man. With him.

Joe didn't have to remember very hard to recall the pain of being dumped by his fiancée. It had laid him low for a long time. His sister had warned him against getting involved with Lydia. He'd ignored her admonition because he hadn't believed the flirtation between them would turn into anything serious.

Now, here was Lydia, suggesting something a lot more permanent between them, something a lot more likely to end up in heartbreak. Joe wasn't sure he should take that kind of chance, especially with a woman as spoiled as Lydia Benedict. She didn't strike him as someone he could count on when times got tough.

On the other hand, there was nowhere he had to be and nothing he needed to do. And if he knew going in that this thing between them was likely to end, he'd be able to guard his heart.

"What is it you suggest I do if I stay?" he asked at last.

Lydia sat up, and he caught his breath at the sight of her pert breasts, with their perfect pink nipples. When she saw the direction of his gaze, she grabbed for the sheet, but he reached out a hand to stop her.

"Don't. Your breasts are beautiful. I want to look."

He wanted to do a lot more than that. His body was giving stiff evidence of just what a randy son of a bitch he was.

She took one look at his avid gaze, blushed, and pulled an edge of the sheet up to cover herself. "I want to have a conversation, Joe. An *uninterrupted* conversation."

Joe laughed and scooted upright so he was sitting with his back against the headboard, then grabbed a corner of the sheet to cover his erection. "Conversation it is."

"As for what you could do if you stayed, you could work with me."

He frowned. "Work for you?"

She shook her head. "No. *With* me. We could learn to be world-renowned investigators together."

"If I'd wanted to be a private investigator, I'd have gone into business with my father," Joe said flatly. A lot of his father's work had involved the sordid side of life, investigating husbands who'd skipped out on paying child support, locating wives who'd stolen away with children, leaving anguished fathers behind, and catching unfaithful husbands and wives in the act. "I have no desire to hunt down cheating husbands and wives."

"We wouldn't be investigating people," she argued. "We'd be looking for stolen art and artifacts. We'd find whatever is missing and return it to its rightful owner."

"Could we make a living doing that?" Joe asked skeptically.

Lydia made a face and gathered the sheet more tightly around her. "I haven't been doing it long enough—or been successful enough—to know the answer to that. But it doesn't matter," she continued doggedly. "Money isn't an issue. I can support both of us very comfortably with the allowance from my trust."

Joe felt a chill run through him. "That's not an option."

He started to rise, in order to dress and get the hell out, but Lydia caught his biceps to hold him in place. He was already imagining her gone from his life, and he didn't like what he saw, so he allowed her feathery touch to hold him in place.

He heard a great deal of bitterness in her voice when she

spoke again.

"It isn't fair, you know."

"What isn't fair?"

She shrugged helplessly. Hopelessly. "I can't help being rich. I can't help the fact that, if I live modestly—or even if I don't—I never need to work a day in my life. Very few of the men I've met will ever have resources equal to mine. Even Harold, wealthy as he is, can't hold a candle to the assets I have in the bank. So no, you and I won't be on the same footing financially. But I can't believe you would condemn me to marrying a man like Harold, because you're too proud to have a rich wife."

"Whoa, lady! Who the hell said anything about marriage?"

Her jaw jutted. "I just did."

Joe jerked his forearm free. "Think again."

"Please, Joe. Don't leave."

The sound of her voice was heart wrenching and held him in place.

She swiped a tear from her cheek and said, "Don't you think we should at least see where this . . . thing . . . between us goes?"

Joe was more than a little tempted. His body had never stopped being aware of her. He was hard and ready, and the last thing he wanted to do was get out of this bed and walk away from her.

"At least stay the night," she urged. "Give yourself time to consider what I'm suggesting."

Joe had never been a fool. And he wasn't going to cut off his nose to spite his face. A beautiful woman had offered to let him spend the night in her bed. Joe gave the response he was certain any red-blooded male would have given.

"I'm all yours, honey. At least until tomorrow morning."

CHAPTER 21

*L*ydia was lying in bed, nestled in Joe's arms, when she awoke to the sound of someone knocking hard on the door of her hotel suite. "Joe," she whispered.

He was instantly awake. "Were you expecting someone?" he asked as he turned on a lamp. He slid out of bed and pulled on his trousers without stopping to put on underwear. He zipped the pants but didn't bother with the button at the top of the fly.

Lydia couldn't take her eyes off of him. She'd traced every scar on his body, studied the play of muscle and sinew and bone, and her hands still itched to touch.

Shirtless, his tux trousers hanging on his hipbones, Joe headed for the door.

Lydia glanced at the clock beside the bed and saw it was nearly midnight. She couldn't imagine who could be calling on her—hunting for her?—at this hour.

Unless it was her father.

Lydia scrambled out of bed, snatched the top sheet to cover her nakedness, and called out to Joe, "Don't open the door!"

Joe paused in mid-stride, turned, and asked, "Why not?"

She stopped in the bedroom doorway and met his gaze with wide, anxious eyes. "It might be my father. In fact, I can't think of anyone else it could be."

Joe raised a brow. "What do you want to do? Whoever it is seems pretty damned determined to see you."

Lydia's heart was beating a wild tattoo. She couldn't bear the thought that her father might think less of her when he discovered Joe in her room. Bull knew that she'd just turned down a wedding proposal from one man, and here she was, already sleeping with another—one she barely knew.

The knocking continued, more insistently.

"We have to do something, honey, or he's going to pound the door down," Joe said.

"Fine!" Lydia replied. She might as well take the bull by the horns. She was a grown woman. She would hold her head high and tell her father that her sex life was none of his business!

She tucked the sheet more tightly around her breasts, then gathered up the tail of cloth dragging behind her and threw it over her arm as though she were wearing a Roman toga. She smiled to herself when she thought how appropriate that comparison was. She crossed to Joe, rose on tiptoe to kiss him—for courage?—then opened the door.

If Joe hadn't been there to catch her, she would have landed in a heap, she was so shocked at the sight that greeted her.

"Good Lord!" she exclaimed when she saw Oliver standing in the hallway. "What are you doing here?"

She felt Joe's arm slide possessively around her waist and felt his body tense for battle. The last thing she wanted was for Joe to end up taking a swing at her brother. She put a restraining hand on his arm and said, "Joe, this is my brother Oliver. Oliver, this is Joe Warren, my . . ." She hesitated, unsure what description applied, and ended up simply saying, "This is Joe."

Oliver stepped inside without being invited to do so, and Lydia let the door slide closed behind him.

A furious blush rose on her cheeks as her brother disdainfully examined first her, and then Joe. The way she and Joe were dressed—or rather, undressed—left nothing to the imagination.

"Is there any way we can speak in private?" Oliver asked, shooting a pointed look at Joe.

"I have a pretty good idea what you're here to say," Lydia replied. "Joe knows what I did."

"He knows that you lied to me? That you betrayed my trust and Mother's trust and nearly caused a priceless gem—for which Mother has great sentimental feeling—to be lost forever?"

Lydia was horribly aware that Joe, with whom she'd hoped to work professionally, was listening to every word of Oliver's venomous but well-deserved condemnation. The guilty knot in her throat made it difficult to speak, but she knew she owed her brother an apology. "I'm sorry," she said in a voice thick with regret.

"Sorry won't cut it!" Oliver said. "How can I ever believe another word you say to me? How can I ever trust you again?"

Lydia heard the deep disappointment in Oliver's voice and felt wretched. She was completely surprised when Joe came to her defense.

"Your sister made a mistake," he said. "Ultimately, there was no harm done. Cut her some slack."

"You have no place in this discussion," Oliver retorted.

"I disagree. I've spent the past couple of days in Lydia's company," Joe replied. "I've had a chance to work with her retrieving the Ghost, and I'd say she's basically an honest and caring person."

Lydia's heart swelled with gratitude for Joe's kind words.

He finished, "I trust her enough that I'm going into business with her."

"Doing what?" Oliver replied in a menacing voice.

Lydia jumped in to deflect Oliver's animosity from Joe to the place where it really belonged: on her. She lifted her chin and said, "Our plans aren't any of your business. Suffice it to say, we're forming a partnership."

Her brother shot her a cynical look. "Is that what they're calling sexual liaisons these days?"

She heard Joe make a growling sound in his throat.

"Who I sleep with is none of your business, either,"

Lydia snapped.

"I thought you were engaged to Harry Delaford," Oliver said.

"Then you were mistaken. Harry asked, but I turned him down."

Oliver focused his gaze on Joe, arched an aristocratic brow, and asked, "Just who are you?"

"Nobody that would matter to you," Joe replied.

"Joe was a soldier," Lydia said, when Joe refused to explain himself. "He left the army because of an injury to his leg."

"Humor me," Oliver said to Lydia. "What kind of business could the two of you possibly run together? Based on Joe's accent, I'm presuming he's an American. Are you planning to move to the States?"

"No," Lydia replied.

"Is Joe planning to move to London?" Oliver asked.

"No," Joe replied, even though the question wasn't directed to him.

Oliver pursed his lips. "Then how—and where—are the two of you going to engage in this business, whatever it is?"

It was a good question. Lydia had wondered herself how she and Joe were going to meld their lives when they lived on different continents. Where would they live when they weren't traveling for work? Where would they settle down and raise their children?

The truth was none of that really mattered right now. She and Joe were at the very beginning of their relationship. They had all the time in the world to figure those things out. She knew all she needed to know: there was something very, very special about Joe Warren. For the first time in her life, Lydia thought that she just might get that fairy tale ending. She just might end up living happily ever after.

Lydia realized she was chewing on a fingernail and yanked her finger from her mouth. "I appreciate your concern, Oliver. Really, I do. But I don't need your help."

"I'm worried that you haven't thought this through." Oliver reached out to lay a big-brotherly hand on Lydia's shoulder, but Joe pivoted with her so that Oliver's hand fell on thin air. Oliver scowled at Joe.

Joe made a dangerous sound in his throat, then said, "Your sister has made her wishes plain. She doesn't want or need your help. You should leave."

For a moment, Oliver looked like he intended to argue the point. Then he focused his gaze on Lydia and said, "I'm always available if you need me."

Oliver was reaching for the door when Lydia cried, "Oliver!"

As he turned back, she pulled herself from Joe's grasp and flung herself into her brother's arms, which opened to receive her. She pressed her cheek against his chest and said, "I truly am sorry, Oliver. I know I've shattered your trust, but I promise you, I will do everything in my power to earn it back."

She pulled her brother's head down, at the same time going up on tiptoe so she could whisper in his ear, "I've found someone I believe I can love. Someone I believe could care for me. Be happy for me."

When she lowered herself again, the crease of worry was still there between his eyes. Lydia felt a pang of disappointment at Oliver's skepticism, his unwillingness to believe that she could have found true love so suddenly, and in such a strange way.

Then he did something completely unexpected. He turned his piercing gaze on Joe and said, "Since you work for Warren and Warren Investigations, I presume this business you and my sister intend to engage in involves investigating?" He'd made it a question, but he didn't wait for an answer. "Especially since I've been aware for some time of Lydia's inclination to follow in my footsteps and search out missing art and artifacts in order to return the items to their rightful owners."

Lydia's brows rose toward her hairline in astonishment. "How did you find out?"

Oliver ignored her, keeping his focus on Joe's ice-blue eyes. "If I'm right, then I have a job for the two of you. I would do it myself, but I'm otherwise engaged at the moment."

Lydia noticed that Oliver didn't explain the project. He waited for Joe to ask what it was. It was a clever way for her brother to get Joe to admit that the work they planned to do was exactly what he suspected.

When Lydia turned to find out Joe's response, she was dumbfounded to find him leaning on the oak cane she'd bought for him. It had been lying in the open box on the coffee table all this time. With no wall to lean on, and apparently unwilling to sit when her brother was standing, Joe must have picked up the cane to support his wounded leg, so he could stay on his feet and remain in the fray.

"I'm listening," Joe said to Oliver.

Lydia crossed to Joe and threaded her arm through his, so they provided a united front to her brother, and said, "We're both listening."

CHAPTER 22

*J*oe couldn't believe how much easier—and less painful—it was to stand with the aid of the oak cane Lydia had bought for him. He'd snatched it out of the box, because it was either prop himself up with something or fall flat on his face. Somehow, with Lydia by his side, using the cane didn't feel so much like he was giving up or giving in. It was more like he was moving on.

"So what's this job you can't do yourself?" he asked Oliver.

"It isn't that I can't. It's just that I'm not interested."

"Why not?

"It isn't art or an artifact that's missing. It's a shipment of gold bullion. The bank is offering a ten percent recovery fee."

"Exactly how much gold is missing?" Joe asked.

"Sixty million."

Joe did the math and whistled. "That's quite a payday." If he and Lydia could find and return the gold, they'd earn *six million* dollars. His half of that would easily allow him to support himself—and a wife—and contribute significantly more to the veterans' organizations he already supported.

Lydia hadn't said anything, and Joe met her gaze, wondering what she was thinking. "I know it isn't exactly what you had in mind," he began.

Lydia turned to her brother and said, "We want the job."

Joe realized he was grinning.

"I'll have my assistant send you the details," Oliver said. He reached out to shake Joe's hand. "Take good care of my sister."

"I will," Joe promised.

He couldn't help seeing the love in Oliver's eyes as Lydia's brother reached out to take both of her hands in his. Oliver leaned down to kiss Lydia's cheek, then chucked her under the chin and said, "Be good. And if you can't be good, for heaven's sake, be careful!"

Lydia laughed, pulled her hands free, and used them to shoo her brother away. "Go! Get out of here! I'm sure you've got something you're looking for somewhere. And we've got a shipment of gold bullion to find."

Oliver left without looking back. Once the door closed behind him, Lydia turned and pressed her face against Joe's chest. He used his free hand to circle her shoulders and pull her close, sliding his hand up beneath her hair to capture her nape. "Are you all right?"

She leaned back to look up at him and let out a shuddering breath. "That could have turned out a lot differently. I feel so

. . . hopeful."

Joe knew what she meant. He felt the same thing, a sort of optimism about the future that he hadn't felt when he'd arrived in Rome such a brief time ago. He leaned down to kiss Lydia, nibbling on her lips, sliding his tongue along the seam until she opened wide for him. His need grew as she returned the favor.

As he kissed his way down her throat toward her breasts, Lydia tugged the sheet free and let it fall to the floor. In a sultry voice she said, "Time for bed."

Joe laughed and said, "Roger that."

$\mathcal{B}$ella sat on the patio of her villa in Greece watching the sun set on an azure sea. She was patting herself on the back at how well everything had turned out. Lydia was in love. And it seemed that Joe Warren was equally smitten.

Bella couldn't have chosen a better man for her only daughter than Lydia had chosen for herself. Not only was Joe Warren a man with tremendous strength of character, he also had the patience to deal with Bella's often-wayward daughter.

Lydia had spent the past forty-five days in Joe's company, the two of them diligently searching for sixty million dollars in stolen gold bullion. Just today, Bella had seen a picture on the Internet of Lydia and Joe smiling happily at each other, the bullion stacked on a table in front of them. Now that they'd found the gold, Bella was convinced it wouldn't be long before Joe declared himself.

Two down. Three to go.

Bella was counting down the days and weeks and months she had left to find spouses for her remaining unwed sons. Time was running short. Her heart had been even less reliable since her encounter in Rome with Bull.

Making love to her husband—and clearing up the ten-year-long misunderstanding between them—had been a joy and a blessing. However, she'd been putting off getting together with Bull ever since, because she was certain that, once he discovered how really bad her heart was, Bull would insist that she rest.

Bella couldn't rest yet. She certainly hadn't been idle over the past forty-five days. She'd contacted Joe Warren's sister, Samantha, and insisted that the young woman come to Greece, so Bella could evaluate whether she wanted to continue using the services of Warren & Warren Investigations. That was a ploy, of course. Bella wanted to vet the young woman as a possible match for her son Riley. At any rate, Bella had provided the first class ticket, and Samantha had accepted the Duchess's invitation.

Bella smiled. Samantha would be arriving about the same time as Riley showed up for a visit. With any luck, Bella could convince Riley to help Samantha look for her missing father. That would give the two young people a chance to get better acquainted with each other—and perhaps to fall in love.

"Your Grace?"

Bella turned to find Emily with a folded blanket clutched to her chest. "I suppose you think I'm going to get a chill once the sun goes down if I don't cover up."

"Yes, Your Grace, I do," Emily said soberly.

"Come on, then. Bring it here."

Emily had been particularly humorless since their return from Rome. Bella couldn't imagine what had happened to make her assistant so glum, unless her large family was badgering her again. "Is everything all right with your brothers and sisters and your parents?" the Duchess asked.

Emily spread the blanket over Bella and tucked it in around her legs. "My family is fine, Your Grace," Emily replied in a dull voice.

"Then what's wrong?"

If it was possible, Emily's pale face got even paler.

Bella patted the lounge chair beside her and moved her legs to make a space for Emily to sit down. "Come here and join me."

"I don't think—"

"I insist."

Once Emily was seated, Bella took the young woman's warm hands in her very cold ones and asked, "Is there anything I can do to help?"

Emily eased her hands free. "No. Nothing."

As Bella watched, a single tear slid down Emily's cheek. "Oh, my dear!" Bella said. "Please tell me what's wrong."

Emily swiped at the tear and managed a wobbly smile. "It's nothing."

"It's certainly something," the Duchess said, "if it's brought someone as strong as you to tears. Come on. Out with it."

"It's just a little heartbreak," Emily said with a rueful twist of her lips.

"Ah," the Duchess said. "The young man doesn't return your feelings?"

Emily shook her head. "No. He doesn't."

"Who is this young man?" Bella asked. "Tell me his name so I can have him drawn and quartered."

Emily chuckled, then pulled a handkerchief from her pocket and blew her nose. "You would be quite dangerous if we were living in medieval times."

"I don't like to see you hurt," Bella said in a quiet voice. "Is there any hope that the young man will change his mind about you?"

Emily looked down at her hands, which clutched the handkerchief. "No chance at all." She lifted her chin and added, "I'm in the mopes now, but I won't allow it to last. I have a life to live, with or without him in it."

"Well said!"

Emily rose, returned the hanky to her pocket, then smoothed her hands down the front of her dress. "Now I need to make sure your dinner is set on the table." She turned and walked away without looking back.

Bella eyed her assistant speculatively. It seemed she would have to live a little bit longer than she'd first thought. Not just *three*, but *four* to go. Her work would not be done until she'd found a man perceptive enough to realize that Emily Sheldon was a woman whose plain looks hid a generous, loving heart. Hmm. Now who could that man be?

ACKNOWLEDGMENTS

I owe a great debt of gratitude to my sister, Joyce Mertens, for proofreading this manuscript. She did the soldier's job of finding all my mistakes. I apologize for any that squeaked through our joint efforts to find and correct them.

I especially want to thank Gail Nelson (www.e-book-design.com) for her willingness to work on a tight deadline to get *Unforgettable* formatted. You are the greatest, Gail!

If you love the cover, thank Nancy November Sloane (nancy@zoomIQ2.com). I certainly do! I couldn't have gotten this book written without Nancy's capable assistance, along with the support of my amazing webmistress, Sally Schoeneweiss (sally@booktalk.com). They make it possible for me to write by keeping all the business elements of this business running smoothly.

Finally, I want to thank you, the reader, for all your support over the twenty-eight years I've been writing romance novels.

You've made me a top ten *New York Times* and *USA TODAY* bestselling author, with more than fifteen million copies of my books in print.

Most of all, your emails, which I personally read, provide the encouragement and support that keep me writing. You can always reach me through my website, www.joanjohnston.com or contact me at www.facebook.com/joanjohnstonauthor. I look forward to hearing from you!

$\mathcal{D}$ear Faithful Reader,

I hope you enjoyed *Unforgettable*, the second book in my Benedict Brothers series of Bitter Creek novels. In case you missed it, the first book in that series, *Invincible*, is available wherever books are sold. *Invincible* features the Duchess of Blackthorne's youngest son, Max Benedict, and FBI agent Kristin Lassiter.

If you'd like to read about the British Benedicts' American cousins, be sure to check out my paperback novel *Outcast*, also available wherever books are sold.

My next paperbook novel, *Sinful*, the first in my King's Brats series of Bitter Creek novels, will be available in stores and online in April 2015. *Sinful* will be followed later in the summer by the next book in the series, *Shameless*.

I'm busy at work on the next Benedict Brothers novel, *Irresistible*, Riley Benedict and Samantha Warren's story. Be sure to sign up for my mailing list at my website, www.joanjohnston. com to receive an e-newsletter announcing when new books will be available. You can also contact me personally through my website or at www.facebook.com/joanjohnstonauthor.

Happy reading,

Joan Johnston

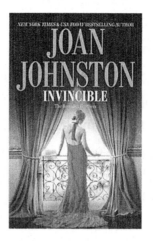

INVINCIBLE

*K*ristin was fighting tears by the time she got to her hotel room. She kicked off her shoes, threw herself onto the bed and hugged a pillow to her chest.

I gave her a kiss for luck.

Why hadn't she asked Max to explain that kiss? How different things might have been! More to the point, why hadn't she contacted Max when she found out she was pregnant? If he'd known they were going to have a child, would he have asked her to marry him? Would he have stepped up and done his share of the parenting?

They'd been teenagers. Kids. Too young to marry. But

still. They'd been good friends. He'd said he cared for her. She'd loved him. Maybe they could have made it. She would never know now. She'd never given him the chance.

Max had been so angry with her tonight. She didn't want to think what he might do if he found out she'd kept the existence of a daughter from him all these years. He wasn't a boy anymore. If he ever found out about Flick, she didn't think he would let her get away with running again.

Was that what she was going to do? Run again?

She'd worn the label *invincible* as a teen on the tennis court, but the truth was, she was a stronger person now than she'd been when those decisions were made. Of course, the self-confidence she'd gained raising a child on her own and pursuing a career that she loved had taken a battering over recent months. But she wasn't anywhere near down and out. She still had plenty of fight left in her.

Kristin swiped at her tears and headed into the bathroom to cleanse the makeup from her face with an inexpensive cold cream. After removing it with a tissue she rinsed with cold water. She looked at her face in the mirror, dripping with water, and didn't like what she saw in her eyes.

Defeat.

The duchess had been wrong. She and Max had discussed what had gone awry between them in the past, but it hadn't resolved anything. Except to make her feel like even more of a fool than she'd felt like ten years ago. Oh, how she wanted to pack her bags, collect her daughter and leave London!

She patted her face dry instead.

If she walked away, she would be leaving without the Blackthorne Rubies. She wanted—she needed—the financial security she would have if she stayed and played that stupid exhibition match.

She resisted the urge to grab her suitcase. She brushed her teeth instead. Which left her staring at herself in the mirror again. And gave her far too much time to think.

It had occurred to her, when she saw Max this morning and realized the powerful physical attraction between them was still there, and tonight, when she'd realized that she wasn't the only one to be hurt by her childish behavior all those years ago, that she'd made a terrible mistake.

She felt wretched, wishing she didn't have to face Max again tomorrow. Especially knowing herself to be in the wrong.

There was something special between us a long time ago. I believe it's still there, beneath all the pain. Maybe Max and I could work through our differences. Maybe we could fall in love again. He could be a father to Flick and we could get married and live happily ever after.

She scoffed. Talk about fairy tales. She might still be attracted to Max, but he obviously didn't feel the same way. She'd seen him kiss Elena tonight. He might be a spy, but he was also still a playboy who used women like tissues and threw them away. She'd better settle for playing the damned exhibition match and not worry about living happily ever after. That special something—the spark between them—had been extinguished.

Liar, liar, pants on fire, a little voice said. *Max might be furious with you. And you might have ruined the possibility of ever living happily ever after with the decision you made to force him out of your life. But the sexual spark isn't gone. He wants you. And, admit it, you want him. So why not seduce him and see what happens?*

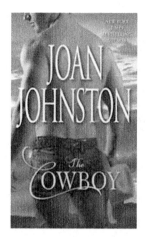

THE COWBOY

"*D*o you remember the last time we danced, Callie?" Trace asked as he moved her around the sawdusted wooden floor to the seductive country tune.

Callie felt her heart skip a beat. She wondered if there was any significance to his question. The last time they had danced was in college, on Valentine's Day. They had left the dance floor that night and driven out into the hill country to a spot along the Colorado River where they could be alone, with only the stars overhead and the cool grass beneath them.

She remembered how much they'd laughed that night, how boyishly Trace had smiled at her in the moonlight, before he pulled her sweater up over her head, leaving her wearing only a plain white bra. It was the only time she had truly regretted being poor. She'd wished she had on some expensive French lingerie, something made of delicate lace that would make her beautiful for him.

Trace hadn't minded. He'd grinned and told her how glad he was that the bra clasp was at her back, because he had an excuse to put his arms around her. He'd made her feel beautiful without the need for rich, expensive things.

That long, lazy night they had spent together on the banks of the Colorado, they'd loved one another with reverence and abandon and delight. She had become a woman in his arms that night. And they had created their son.

"I remember," she murmured.

"I found you enchanting, Callie." He turned her in a circle that forced their bodies close.

Callie barely had time to register the fact that he'd phrased his compliment in the past tense before he added, "You look tired."

"It's been a long day," she said, aggravated that she could feel hurt that he no longer found her enchanting. She kept her eyes determinedly focused over his shoulder. She considered staying silent, but decided it would be safer to direct the conversation herself. "Congratulations on winning the bid on the number twenty-three animal. Smart Little Doc was a steal at $76,000."

"That colt you got wasn't bad, either," he said.

"You mean the one colt you let me have." Callie bit her tongue to keep from saying more.

"I didn't expect you to return after you left the stands," Trace said. "Why did you?"

"My father called me a quitter."

He hesitated, then said, "And you're not?"

"You left me, Trace, not the other way around."

"And now I'm back," he said quietly.

"You've been back nearly four months," she said, her eyes flashing. "Today is the first I've seen of you. Am I supposed to fall at your feet—or into your bed? I'm a widow now, the mother of two children."

His jaw flexed. "I'm not likely to forget either condition. That doesn't change the fact that I still find you desirable."

"But not enchanting?" Callie flushed as she realized what she'd revealed.

"I never said you weren't enchanting, Callie," he said as he met her gaze. "I merely observed that you look tired, which you do. You've obviously been working too hard. I could make life easier for you, if you'd let me."

"More Blackthorne charity?" I don't need it, and I don't want it."

"You may not want it. But you need it," Trace contradicted.

Callie refused to argue the point.

"Since Dusty's bum leg put him out of business, I need someone to train my new stud for the Futurity," he said. "I'll pay you a premium wage for your time and half the purse, if Smart Little Doc finishes in the top ten."

"I will never, ever work for you."

"Don't make promises you can't keep, Callie." He pulled her close so her breasts grazed his chest.

She pushed at his shoulder, caught a neighbor watching with raised brows, and muttered, "Let me go, Trace."

"The dance isn't over, Callie."

He might as well have said, *I'm not done with you.* She'd gotten the message loud and clear. "We don't know each other anymore, Trace. We might as well be strangers."

"I know you in every way there is for a man to know a woman."

"I've changed," she said. "I'm not the girl who fell foolishly in love with you."

His eyes focused intently on her. "So much the better."

"What do you want from me?"

"That should be obvious."

His hand pressed against the small of her back, drawing her close enough to feel his hardness against her softness. A frisson of awareness streaked through her. She gasped, tried to catch the sound, but was too late.

"Look at me, Callie," he commanded.

Callie tried to jerk free, but Trace tightened his hold. She raised her chin and glared at him. "Whatever we had between us is over and done."

"Not quite," he said.

She eyed him warily, her heart thumping crazily. "What is that supposed to mean?"

"I haven't had my fill of you."

She snorted derisively. "You make me sound like a bottle of beer you haven't finished swilling."

His voice was low and seductive. "I was thinking of something utterly soft and incredibly sweet I haven't finished sampling."

Callie felt the flush creeping up her throat but could do nothing to stop it. "I don't love you anymore, Trace."

"Who said anything about love?"

ABOUT THE AUTHOR

*J*oan Johnston is the top ten *New York Times* and *USA TODAY* bestselling author of more than 50 novels and novellas with more than 15 million copies of her books in print. Joan has an eclectic background and worked as a director of theater, drama critic, newspaper editor, college professor, and attorney on her way to becoming a full-time author.

Joan has a B.A. in Theater Arts from Jacksonville University, Jacksonville, Florida, and an M.A. in Theatre from the University of Illinois in Urbana. Joan also earned a J.D. with honors from the University of Texas at Austin. She worked as an attorney for Hunton & Williams in Richmond, Virginia, and Squire, Sanders, and Dempsey in Miami, Florida.

As an Air Force brat, Joan traveled the world from North Africa to North Dakota. She visited Marrakech and learned to ride on an Arabian stallion in Morocco, and collected cowrie shells and let an octopus play on her hand at Lingayan Gulf in the Philippines. She grew up in a family of seven kids, which influenced her to write family sagas like her Bitter Creek and Hawk's Way series.

Joan plays tennis, hikes, and attends as many Denver Broncos games as she can in between research trips around the world. She lives in Colorado.

You can reach Joan through her website, www.joanjohnston.com, through Facebook at www.facebook.com/joanjohnstonauthor or on Twitter at twitter.com/joanjohnston.

CPSIA information can be obtained
at www.ICGtesting.com
Printed in the USA
LVOW04s0741101016
507659LV00003B/135/P